THURS	FRI	SAT
O	**2** WHORE WEASEL'S DAY	**13**	**4** HOSPITAL UMBLES SALE
	1ST DAY OF **9** DISSENSION	2ND DAY OF **13** DISSENSION	DISSENSION OF **11** DISSENSION
5 ...RKET	**16**	**13**	**18** ST. BLOW GHERKIN'S
2 ...DRIVE	**23**	**13**	**25**
9 ...ON	**30** COVEN OPEN-DAY	**13**	ECTOPLASM COLLECTION WILL NOW ONLY BE FORTNIGHTLY

Dear Megan,

I got you this weird look because I thor
You will like it + I love you.

Love,
Thea

a Scarfolk Books book

Discovering Scarfolk

For tourists & other trespassers

10 9 8 7

Ebury Press, an imprint of Ebury Publishing,
20 Vauxhall Bridge Road,
London SW1V 2SA

Ebury Publishing is part of the Penguin Random House group of companies
whose addresses can be found at global.penguinrandomhouse.com

First published by Ebury Press in 2014
www.penguin.co.uk

A CIP catalogue record for this book is available from the British Library

ISBN: 9780091958480

Designer: Estuary English and Two Associates
Editor: Angela Herlihy
Picture research: Sarah Hopper and Claire Gouldstone

Printed and bound in Italy by L.E.G.O. S.p.A

Penguin Random House is committed to a sustainable future for our business,
our readers and our planet. This book is made from Forest Stewardship
Council® certified paper.

a Scarfolk Books book

Discovering
Scarfolk

For tourists & other trespassers

Richard Littler

EBURY
PRESS

Introduction

by Dr Ben Motte

(Editor, *International Journal of Cultural Taxidermy*)

'The past is a foreign country: they do things differently there, so I wouldn't recommend it as a holiday destination.'

J.K. Schaim (after L.P. Hartley)

THE BOOK YOU have in your hands contains a selection of archival materials pertaining to Scarfolk, a town in North West England, which is just west of northern England, though its precise location is unknown.

The archive is equally imprecise, unlike one methodically collated and carefully maintained by an official body such as a museum, notable person's estate, or child exchange farm. At first glance, one could dismiss the archive's contents as a meandering assemblage of print ephemera from the 1970s but that would belittle its historical and cultural significance. The artefacts collected here permit us access to Britain's recent social attitudes and mores, many of which – we may be surprised to discover – we had either forgotten or suppressed.

Before I discuss the artefacts' sociological implications, I see it as my duty to bring to your attention how I came by the contents of this book. As a historian and academic, I eschew irrational notions so it is with some reluctance that I describe the circumstances as a mystery, an enigma that has consumed a substantial portion of my time.

Several months ago, I received in the post a large parcel wrapped in several sheets of reused brown paper. Enclosed was a 1970s' tourist guide entitled *Discovering Scarfolk*. Many of the book's pages are missing and the surviving ones are rubbed soft from frequent reading. The once slender volume is swollen to many times its original size and the spine, barely held together by layers of yellowing, brittle sticky tape, has deformed to accommodate numerous inserted documents and scraps: newspaper reports, public information literature, council documents, advertisements, book covers, product packaging, record sleeves, leaflets, till receipts for everyday products such as jam and magnetised crucifixion pyjamas and other print matter of varying size, shape and colour. Though I now refer to it as 'the archive', when I first laid eyes on this haphazard collection of papers I thought that it had been mistakenly diverted from its true destination: a paper recycling facility.

Only when I scrutinised the well-thumbed items did I discover that many were accompanied by often nonsensical annotations. For example, here is one of the first I encountered:

> […] The many drinking straws protruding from the library walls are not art – they're for breathing – has Mrs P imprisoned children in the walls? And does she hide [illegible words] inside her prosthetic leg?[1]

As I read on, drawn in by the cryptic texts and images, I realised that I knew the author of these feverish commentaries. His name was Daniel Bush and he had been a fellow student when we read Telepathic Journalism at St Cheggers Pop Christ College, London, in the late 1960s.

If that was not unsettling enough, when I decided to expand my research into Scarfolk, I found only scant references to the town, and deeper investigation resulted only in further perplexity. There was nothing in the records of the British Library and a Google search produced only limited, unhelpful results. I also realised that, though I had always been aware of Scarfolk, I had never actually visited it in person, nor did I know anyone from the town. I spoke to friends and colleagues, all of whom said the same.

[1.] To clarify: the authorial insertion is not meant to be taken literally or imply that illegible words themselves were hidden inside 'Mrs P's' leg. Furthermore, due to advancements in medical technology, by 1970 it was no longer physically possible to hide such words in any form of prosthesis. For reference, here are several attempts at rendering illegible words: poonty, boloques, juffmunch, carpoo, snazellfonks.

Furthermore, I found that Scarfolk was not on any map of Britain I examined, though it does appear in several encyclopaedias, *Oxblood's Encyclopaedia*[2] and *The Daisyhorror History of the Past*[3] to name but two. Oddly, in all cases the brief entries are identical, seem to have been written by the same person and appeared only for the first time in 1970 editions.

which was sometimes used in the manufacture of dirty things.
SCARFOLK. A small town, depending on the size of the town it is compared to, and how broad one's definition of 'town' is. It is located in the same region as several nearby towns and populated by many of its own residents, most of who live in the town. The name is a conflation of two ancient, pre-language words, 'Skarfo' and 'lk,' which roughly translate as 'the place that is avoided by eels'. This probably refers to the great eel cull of 451BCE (eels were once believed to be pickpockets). The town was founded in the 4th century by the ascetic monk Saint Jeff who is now better known for inventing the *cocta ovum parum acetabulum*, literally 'little spoon for a boiled-egg'.
SCARFPIN. A pin used to hold a tie in place or secure a child to a noticeboard. Also used in witchcraft by crafty witches.

Apart from these nebulous snippets no other facts are included; no description of the town's precise co-ordinates, no detailed population figures or socio-economic details. In fact, I found no other *verifiable* reference to Scarfolk's existence before 1970, nor any reference to it after 1979. However, there is an entry for a 'Scarefolke' in the *Domesday Book* of 1086CE. The details are meagre, cryptic, if not downright baffling. A typical *Domesday Book* entry[4] lists amount of plough land and taxable resources, among other details, but the 'Scarefolke' entry simply reads:

[2.] *Oxblood's Encyclopaedia*. First published and compiled in 1804 by known fraudster and confidence trickster, Robert Jamboree, who also produced England's first pornographic publication, *Consumptive Courtesans Weakly*.

[3.] *The Daisyhorror History of the Past*, first published in 1946, was compiled by 11-year-old schoolgirl Nancy Friend, who was accused by some of actually being 63-year-old Hans Arschlachs, a Nazi war criminal who disappeared in 1945.

[…] In the name of William of England, the Lord God, and the fucking [illegible word. Looks like 'pineapple'], and for the benefit of all, let no good man attend this land for fear of the unholy *Ritel* [5][sic].

[Translated from Old English by J. Scud, an old English translator.]

There is no way of ascertaining if this is indeed the same Scarfolk. The only thing we can rely on for sure is Daniel Bush's Scarfolk archive – still the only tangible testimony to the town's existence. Yes, I insist on the use of the word 'tangible.' Can one man really have forged all these documents and within them an internally consistent town with distinct people, working businesses, schools, social clubs, not to mention rife but unhealthy attitudes towards race, gender, children and synchronised swimmers?

However, accepting the credibility of Daniel Bush's archive is a disturbing prospect. If we entertain the notion that Scarfolk is real, we are faced with innumerable implications.

Did we really permit the electrification of the water supply? Can it be true that we had no misgivings as we fried, baked, boiled and poached our least interesting children or made them fight in pits for our entertainment?[6] Did we really monitor the very thoughts of our own citizens? Finally, could these once acceptable but now disdained ideals still be a part of our cultural DNA?

[4.] Other information usually includes: number of talking livestock; number of resident witches; number of weasels used as soft furnishings; amount of ergot harvested.

[5.] The meaning of 'Ritel' was not recorded. However, not only do artefacts in Daniel Bush's archive allude to the identity of the cryptic 'Ritel', they also cast light on who or what might have been at the dark heart of this mysterious town.

[6.] Parents encouraged their children to join after-school clubs such as Thump Chums UK, which was modelled on the Boy Scout movement. The first rule of Thump Chums was 'you can talk about Thump Chums to whoever you like as long as you thump them'. Children were frequently sent on organised trips to Northern Ireland so that they could take part in the Troubles. However, most young people opposed physical conflict, partly because they lacked a rudimentary sense of enjoyment.

Heard the buzz?

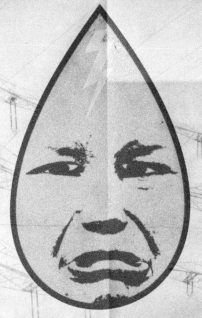

From 21th March, 1974

Your local authority will be introducing electricity to the water supply

Clean, free, odourless, and yellow, electricity has been scientifically proven to halve the number of teeth in children and can be effectively used to maintain control in the classroom.

DON'T FLUSH YOUR CHILD'S FUTURE AWAY

Water Electrification

For more information please reread this poster Scarfolk Council Water Boarding

A poster preparing citizens for the imminent electrification of the water supply.

The archive addresses more than just social conventions. It is also a highly personal one that, like Theseus's twine, guides the reader around a labyrinth, and somewhere in that maze is the answer to a question that one man obsessively fought to answer for many years:

WHO OR WHAT TOOK MY SONS?

In this volume I have attempted to order Daniel Bush's archive and hopefully convey to you as succinctly as possible what I feel he was trying to communicate. I am aware that I could have approached the material in numerous ways, but I hope I have chosen the most scholarly. As difficult as it may be, I recommend you do the same as you enter the world of Daniel Bush and discover Scarfolk for yourself.

Dr Ben Motte (6.6.1944–6.6.2014)

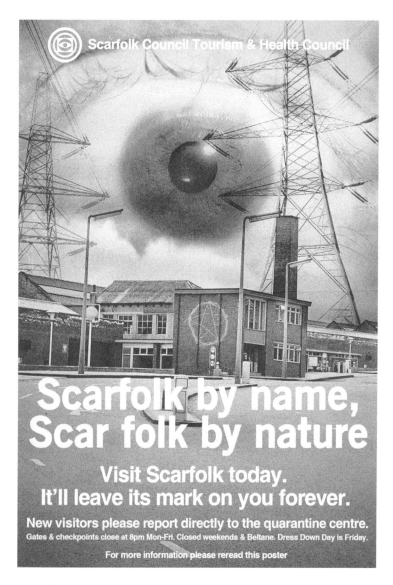

A Scarfolk tourism poster, 1972.

Disappearance Day

DESPITE THE CHAOS of Daniel's archive, one thing is clear: it points to the events of 23 December 1970, which is when Daniel and his two young twins, Joe and Oliver, planned to move house. According to his notes their day started early. Having sold his house (for well below the estimate),[7] Daniel packed his boys into a removal van and took the M13 heading north. His destination was the semi-rural northern town of Sedaton where he had bought a new house in a community for victims of artistic and cultural works (see 'Who is Daniel Bush?', p. 22).

It is only a nine-hour drive but the family never arrived.

In researching this book I drove the same route. On the way, the Bushes would have passed several major towns and cities: Stumpton, the birthplace of Harold Pug, the first man in Britain to climb a tree for pleasure; and Cockchester (pronounced Dickchester), well known for its legends of raining frogs, fish and Shetland ponies. He would also have driven through the Midlands Hedge which once separated the south from the north in an attempt to confine rabies to the latter.

---

[7] The average price for an average house for a below-average family in Scarfolk in 1970 was £4,995. Average families with 2.5 children were advised to discard the half child to alleviate the burden on the Notional Health Service. By 1976, millions of incomplete children were homeless and, following a public outcry in 1979, a charity called Better Half was set up. Better Half maintained a vast database of half children with the intention of locating ideal other halves. The scheme was successful and many sets of half children were surgically conjoined. However, 'double acts', as they were colloquially known, soon discovered that their social benefits had been halved because they were now, in the eyes of the government, one person. Unfortunately, not all laws were updated concurrently and for a long time a 'double act' could not marry another person for fear of being prosecuted for bigamy.

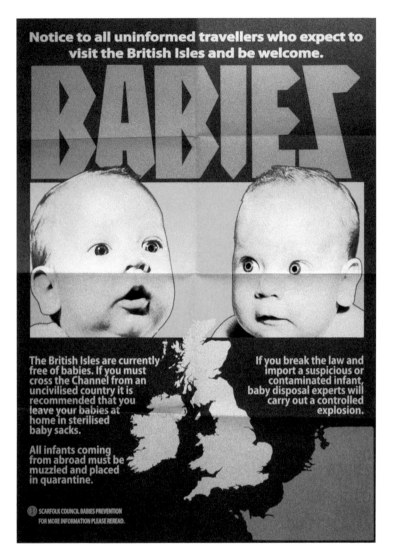

Due to appalling literacy, thousands of southern rabbis, rabbits and babies were separated from their families and communities and sent north of the Midlands Hedge.

After the Hedge there is an uninterrupted 100-mile stretch of industrial estates: logistics companies and warehouses; electrical substations; meat-packing and funeral homes and the like. There are few places to stop and one can imagine that after several hours on the road Daniel and the boys would have needed a break to stretch their legs, use the toilet, grab a bite to eat and get a quick roadside vaccination.

Daniel's most reasonable option would have been to visit the town of Easby, which is well known throughout Britain for being, as the town's tourist literature states, 'The place to stop for lunch if you've been driving for many hours to a new home with two young boys.'

However, Daniel instead made the questionable decision to drive to Scarfolk. We know this because his archive contains a selection of identifiable objects from the fast-food chain restaurant Quimpy: a menu, an unopened sachet of transparent sad-dog sauce and a receipt.

After lunch, according to Daniel's notes, he and the boys went to a local chemist where Daniel tried to refill a prescription for medication he had misplaced called Lobottymed, which is given to chronic depressives and, occasionally, to arrogant cattle. However, without a prescription from a doctor, the pharmacist refused to help the increasingly agitated Daniel, stating that he was legally authorised only to offer him an NHS 10-minute trepanning session and/or a gristle-free raspberry lolly.

Daniel and the boys were soon on the road again heading through the wasteland of industrial buildings towards their final destination, but 10 minutes outside Scarfolk, Oliver, the smaller of the twins, wanted to go the toilet. They pulled into a remote, single-pump Testicoil petrol station. Daniel writes:

> Joe and Oliver ran inside to use the toilet while I searched again in the back of the van for my medication. It was a needle in a haystack. I recall there was a dinner service, a fondue set, a cuddly toy, a teasmade, attractive garden furniture, a selection of Continental wines, hair curlers, a stereo music centre, but no medication. I did find our white-and-red medicine box but it was full of Oliver's toys, including his favourite dinosaur.

A Quimpy Burger menu. This fast-food outlet served fast food made in the popular, lazy, insanitary American style.

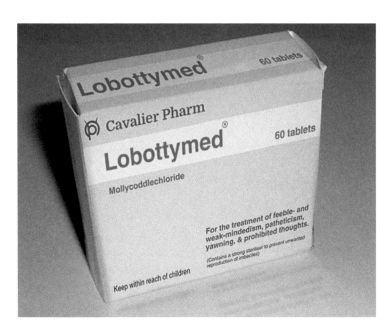

Lobottymed. Made from a protein released by the brains of surprised simpletons when they are unexpectedly slapped.

Testicoil Oil. Founded by cocktail umbrella magnate Ben Greade in 1947.

Several minutes later the boys had still not returned and Daniel went after them. As he entered the service station it was plunged into darkness: yet another strike by the NUDE. Daniel writes:

> I found the petrol station manager, Trevor Vestige, lighting dozens of candles.[8] I asked him where the toilets were but I was told there weren't any such facilities. When he claimed not to have seen any boys I felt the first tremors of panic.
>
> I called out their names. Silence. I made Vestige take me around the back, but there was only a small office, hardly big enough to contain the desk and polystyrene pentangle that dominated it. There was also a narrow corridor, the walls of which were lined with disordered stacks of replacement windscreen wipers, cans of de-icer and those ectoplasm car ornaments that dangle from the rear-view mirror and shout out random messages from beyond the grave.
>
> Joe and Oliver were nowhere to be found. I checked the perimeter of the petrol station but there was no sign of them. The neighbouring warehouses were all empty and abandoned. Beyond was scrubland, row upon row of chain fencing and fields of pylons, like a petrified steel forest stretching into the pale winter horizon.

Daniel spent two more panicked hours in dwindling light scouring the vicinity to no avail. He decided to return to Scarfolk to report the missing boys. Vestige agreed to keep the petrol station open until his return in case the boys turned up.

[8.] Vestige was no stranger to fire-related risk. He had been previously arrested for igniting a tortoise during an illegal, high-stakes game of croquet.

In a dispute over having to pay for their own pedicures, the National Union of Darkness Eradicators (NUDE), which provided the nation's light, went on strike on numerous occasions between 1970 and 1976. In an effort to conserve dwindling light resources, the government asked the people of Britain to close their eyes when they were not using them.

Wanted balloon posters published by the Department of Justice Prevention.

I got back to Scarfolk by 6pm. The strike was still in effect
and the town was in shadows. Only car headlights, torches
and distant hillside pyres pierced the blackness.

Daniel drove directly to the police station. The officer on duty, PC James
Lyre, took down his details but warned him that there was nothing he could
do until the strike ended and the electricity was switched back on, especially
because several officers were nyctophobic. Daniel wrote:

In the light of gas lamps, I noticed two policemen on the
other side of the room repeatedly glance in my direction
and share a private giggle. I implored officer Lyre to
return with me to the petrol station, but he was curiously
reluctant and blushed like a schoolgirl.[9]

Frustrated, Daniel returned alone to the petrol station to discover that,
though electricity had been restored, the station was closed. There was
no sign of Vestige. Daniel resumed his search of the area but it was futile
in the dark. He had no choice but to wait in the cab of his removal van
and resume his search at first light. He found no sign of the boys. Instead,
he encountered something that disturbed him. Across the petrol station
forecourt and the surrounding desolate scrubland, innumerable shiny new
metal staples littered the ground. Additionally, the wind whipped up little
eddies of discarded hole-punch paper discs.

Daniel was soon distracted by the arrival of PC Lyre and a middle-
aged man who was introduced as Dr Hushson. Daniel began to elaborate
about the disturbing significance of the out-of-context stationery supplies
(for reasons that will become clear later) but he found the men 'somewhat
indifferent, almost distracted'. Daniel writes:

[9.] Though Daniel's paranoia over the policemen's reactions is understandable,
the following should also be taken into consideration. Until 1979 the blue dye in
policemen's uniforms contained a plant extract found to be a hallucinogen. It was
banned when several hundred policemen across the country believed that they
had been ordered to arrest balloons, which not only almost caused a collapse of
the party accessory industry but also meant that millions of pounds were spent
on building prisons for the balloons, the vast majority of which were completely
innocent. This may have been a reason for the policemen's odd behaviour.

It soon dawned on me that they didn't believe me. Again
and again, they emphasised that no one had actually seen
my boys, and I realised why the doctor was present: They
thought I was insane; they didn't believe that Joe and
Oliver really existed...

Daniel was cold, he had not slept, nor had he eaten anything since
lunch the previous day; he had probably not even had a poo. More than
anything he was sickened by anxiety, so this implication from two men he
was relying on in his moment of desperate need must have struck him as
nightmarish. Daniel writes in his notes that he snapped and railed at their
unprofessionalism. Like the chemist, the doctor offered him a raspberry
lolly to appease him, and the policeman asked Daniel if he would like to
see a soothing card trick, which only made Daniel angrier. At this point, it
became obvious to an exasperated Daniel that only tangible evidence would
conciliate the two men.

But as I rooted through the many boxes and bags my
heart collapsed into the pit of my stomach. I couldn't find
a single possession of the boys. Even the red-and-white
box containing Oliver's toy dinosaur that I'd seen only the
day before now contained nothing but medical supplies:
bandages, a home-anaesthetic kit and jars of Wichs
Blindness Ointment made by Cavalier Pharm.

Coincidentally (or otherwise) it was another Cavalier Pharm product that is
controversial in this case.

The doctor informed me that he had spoken to the
pharmacist I visited the day before. He knew what med
ication I was taking [Lobottymed] and went into great
detail about the adverse side-effects of sudden withdrawal
– memory loss, delusions, mental confusion, two lovely
little yellow chaffinches and memory loss – which can be
influenced by genuine trauma from the past.

Daniel in turns pleaded with the men and berated them for believing he could fabricate the fully-fleshed-out and consistent lives of two young boys. It is the first time in Daniel's notes that he hints at a potential unpleasantness below the skin of this average British town: 'A less sensible person could have been excused for suggesting a conspiracy.'

But before we defame the town and some of its respected figures, and become mired in convenient inaccuracies and half-truths, let us be as thorough as possible. Can and should doubt be cast over Daniel's account? We can certainly appreciate the perspective of the two sceptical, albeit sympathetic professionals. After all, Daniel by his own admission had not taken his medication for more than a day. He could not provide any evidence of his boys' existence and there is a deep and painful trauma in his past, which I feel must be included here.

The following information about Daniel is not directly touched upon in the archive; I have only discovered it through my own research. It is not much to go on, but it gives us an insight into the mind of Daniel Bush, something that Dr Hushson suggested was at the root of the mystery.

Wichs EyeRub, manufactured by Scarfolk pharmaceutical firm Cavalier Pharm, was rubbed into children's eyes to temporarily blind them while their parents did things they did not want their children to see. However, it was recalled after an unforeseen side-effect caused a class of children to escape from a high-security infant school posing as alarmed peahens.

Who is Daniel Bush?

 THE FOLLOWING BIOGRAPHICAL information may have some bearing on what occurred following the events of Christmas 1970.

On 6 January 1963, at St Poodlestain's church in West Eastcake, Daniel married Joy Tyburn, a Tuber Psychologist who worked as a farm therapist counselling root crops with learning difficulties. A year later, Joy gave birth to the couple's twins, Joe and Oliver. The birth was hard but only light medicinal guesswork was required. There is nothing to suggest that, for the first years of the young family's life, they were anything but happy. Daniel was by now a journalist writing for a local newspaper, *The Daily Day*, and Joy was working towards a doctorate, focusing on impulsive behaviour in the King Edward.

However, Daniel's world was turned upside down on 6 January 1969 – Daniel and Joy's wedding anniversary – when tragedy struck for the second time in his life.[10]

There is an extant police report, written by an attending officer, which describes what happened in detail.

[10.] Reports show that in 1956 Daniel's adoptive parents were killed in a candy floss-related accident at the famous seaside resort of Southporn-on-Sea. According to the court hearing, Jake French, the man who owned the candy floss stand, had long dreamt of making his mark in the glitzy, highly-competitive world of seaside snacks. When he announced his new Never-Ending Candy Floss he won the praise he had long strived for. However, his new-found celebrity turned sour when his secret recipe was found to contain very little sugar but quite a lot of fibreglass.

TOWNTON POLICE

Telephone: Townton 786876

Our Ref: HJX-7B

Case #: 001

Name/Rank:▓▓▓▓▓▓

Police Station
Townton Street
Townton
TO11 1TN

6 Jan, 1969

I arrived at Maggotty Road at about 1700hrs with Constable C▓▓▓▓
There we discovered the prostrate body of Mrs Bush who had
unfortunately succumbed to a state of deceasementisationism.

A small crowd had gathered around the body. Mr Bush was emotionally
overwrought and had to be restrained by Constable ▓▓▓▓, who
endeavoured to distract the grieving man with a magic card trick,
while I attempted to resuscitate Mrs Bush.

This I found particularly difficult because just prior to the
incident, myself and Constable ▓▓▓▓ had enjoyed a bag of chips and a
jumbo sausage and was suffering from synchronous diaphragmatic
flutters (hiccups).

I asked Constable ▓▓▓▓ to take over from me and I completed the
magic trick in his stead. However, given the circumstances, I didn't
perform as well as I might. I bungled the trick's conclusion and as a
consequence Mr Bush wasn't any less agitated than when we arrived; in
fact, he may have been more distressed. Additionally, Constable ▓▓▓▓
could not complete the resuscitation procedure because Mrs Bush's
hair repeatedly touched his face and made him 'feel all tickly'.

Luckily, a large group of school children were passing, each
holding a balloon. Constable ▓▓▓▓ lined up the children in single
file and instructed them to sing the nursery rhyme 'Doctor Foster
Went to Gloucester' while, one by one, at the end of each stanza,
they squeezed the contents of their balloons into Mrs Bush's mouth.

Constable ▓▓▓▓ returned to Mr Bush who by now was weeping
uncontrollably and, in my opinion, a little selfishly given how much
effort we had put into the magic trick. I turned my attention to the
gathered crowd to seek out potential witnesses.

According to one eye-witness, a Mrs Baggott of 12 Flay Street, Mr and
Mrs Bush...

> '...were crossing the road when, suddenly, out of
> nowhere, there was a troupe of Morris dancers...

OVER--

...They were all over the road, not paying any attention to other traffic or pedestrians. The couple (Mr and Mrs Bush) was caught in the path of the dancers, who made no effort whatsoever to avoid clashing with them. The dancers ploughed right into them and the lady [Mrs Bush] was trampled to the ground. All I could hear was the jingling of little bells. It was terrifying.'

Another bystander, Mr Ken Know of 16 Have Ave, reported a potentially relevant detail:

'I know for a fact that the Morris dancers aren't from around here. Also, their handkerchiefs weren't standard kit. In fact, I'll put money on them being illegal. That's probably why they didn't stop.'

He went on to say that:

'There was also the horrific smell of cider...'

All bystanders also confirmed briefly seeing, on the other side of the road, a faceless figure, 8- or 9-feet tall with horns, covered from head-to-toe in animal furs.

Witnesses were then distracted by the tragedy, but when they looked back the figure was gone.

In his place there were hundreds of staples, paperclips and tiny paper discs like those discarded from an office hole-punch machine.

Despite the efforts of the police (and local schoolchildren), Joy Bush was pronounced dead at the scene at 5.66pm.

The following day a report appeared on page two of *The Daily Day*. It is surprisingly perfunctory considering that Daniel Bush was a staff journalist at the newspaper.

> MRS JOY BUSH, 27, was killed yesterday in a hit-and-run folk-dancing accident. She is outlived by her husband and two young sons. Police are advising the public to call 999 if they hear any unfamiliar bells, unexpectedly smell cider or see anyone in possession of a prohibited handkerchief.

We may never learn who the Morris dancers were. Even more mysterious is the fur-clad figure. How does such an entity walk leisurely along a busy road in the centre of a medium-sized town and then disappear without a trace? Daniel suspected that the stationery supplies he found at the site of

Local TV stations broadcast public information warnings about rogue Morris dancers.

his boys' disappearance may have been connected to those found at the time of his wife's death.

Dry reports and official statements are not required to empathise with the devastated young family: Daniel was a man struggling to overcome his own grief to raise two doubtlessly distressed and mourning children. He was also fired by *The Daily Day* after writing a paranoid article that accused the Women's Institute of systematic brainwashing and spiking Shingles cakes, tins of boiled auntmeat and breadless sandwiches with elephant tranquillisers. It is not at all surprising that he was prescribed Lobottymed.

Mr Rudyard Shingles Cakes, 1970s.

Raw emotions aside, one pertinent fact that I did unearth reveals that Joy's newspaper obituary, which mentions Joe and Oliver, is corroborated by a school enrolment record: Joe and Oliver, or 'the Bush twin' [sic] clearly existed. They continued to attend their local school, but in November 1970 they were removed by Daniel, never to return. Over the course of the next two weeks Daniel planned his family's move to the rural northern town of Sedaton where he had bought a new house. As we now know, they never arrived.

The Town's Response to the Disappearance

GRANTED, DANIEL SUFFERED mental health problems after Joy's death, but in a later diary entry he appears more stable. He had also undergone a radical form of cognitive therapy during which patients are encouraged to repeatedly draw a detailed sketch of their mind, re-imagined as a large mansion with each room guarded by a well-trained guard goose.[11]

> It was a difficult time but the medication and therapy got me back on an even keel. When I made the decision to move house I wasn't running away. It was a calm decision. We had discussed it at length. As a family.

Even a well-balanced person without Daniel's troubled history could be excused for the emotional reaction to the events that he experienced in Scarfolk.

On the afternoon following the disappearance of Joe and Oliver Bush, after Daniel's confrontation with Dr Hushson and PC Lyre outside the Testicoil petrol station, a report appeared in the Scarfolk Herald (see p. 184, Appendix I, for the full article).

[11.] Dr Brownest, a colleague of mine, explained to me that visualisation exercises are a standard part of a patient's treatment. They allow the patient to psychologically 'clean and decorate' each room in turn, affording him feelings of control over his life. However, in the mid-1970s the treatment came under scrutiny when gangs of organised psychics started breaking into patients' 'mental mansions', stealing millions of pounds' worth of suppressed memories and expensive kitchenware.

An unnamed girl called Julie Barnes reads the issue of the Scarfolk Herald *which features the article about Joe and Oliver's disappearance.*

Scarfolk Herald / 22.12.1970 / Missing Bush boys

Daniel came by a copy of a photograph that was taken by a Scarfolk Herald *staff photographer. The figures placed in the scene are wearing the same clothes that Joe and Oliver were wearing. It was as if the boys had originally been in the photograph but were later removed. Additionally, the photograph was recorded to have been taken on the 22nd of December, the day before their actual disappearance.*

As much as the article alerts the community to the disappearance, it is also too vague to be of much benefit. It reads like a journalistic template.[12] Were crucial details omitted simply because the author did not believe the story to be credible, or did he deliberately divert and misdirect? And there are other questions: how did the article's author know about Joy's demise? How did he know that one of the boys had a mole on one of his kidneys? How did he know that neither boy owned a pig? (Again, see Appendix I.)

If there are any lingering doubts about the events presented thus far being the

---

[12.] Journalism templates were frequently used throughout the 1970s, especially for popular reports involving crime and supernatural occurrences. Newspapers printed the articles but left spaces in the text for the reader to add their own details. This way news could be personalised.

product of a troubled mind, a prank, or even an unfortunate misunderstanding, the next development in Daniel's story is sure to dispel them.

> In the dim, early morning light, at the service station on the outskirts of Scarfolk, I was determined to prove that my boys existed. I insisted that Dr Hushson and PC Lyre accompany me back to Scarfolk.

With the polite but disinclined men in tow, Daniel retraced his steps, returning first to Quimpy Burger. Diane Heidem, the waitress, claimed not to have seen Daniel with any children. Daniel later noted down everything she said: 'I didn't see any kids. There may have been a couple of dwarves, but they were big ones: at least six feet tall.'

Furthermore, Heidem asserted that Daniel ate alone; he ordered and paid for only one meal. She was quite certain of it. '[Daniel Bush] was talking to himself. Or maybe to someone who wasn't there. Or maybe they had been there but left and [Daniel Bush] either hadn't noticed or had forgotten to stop talking.'

Receipts were produced and compared and she and Daniel argued about how much was paid and for what. However, both Daniel's and the restaurant's till receipts were ambiguous due to poor printing. Heidem also produced a polaroid photograph of Daniel eating alone (she had, by chance, just bought a polaroid camera and was experimenting) as well as a sketch by an official court artist, who just happened to be dining at the same time and left it behind. While compelling, these proofs are strangely convenient.

Daniel was met with a similar response at the chemist's and, while I do not wish to put words in his mouth, I speculate that he must have struggled to contain his swelling anxiety as, one by one, townspeople appeared to corroborate the doctor's theory that Joe and Oliver were figments of his imagination, manifested by a negative withdrawal from his medication. Indeed, Daniel wrote in his notes:

> I struggled to contain my swelling anxiety as, one by one, townspeople appeared to corroborate the doctor's theory that Joe and Oliver were figments of my imagination, manifested by a negative withdrawal from my medication.

The doctor ordered the pharmacist to repeat Daniel's prescription, reasoning that if his children truly did exist, the only way Daniel would be able to make the authorities believe him is if they could rule out any delusions caused by his withdrawal.

> When I started shouting and accusing the whole town of
> conspiracy, of harbouring Morris dancers and horned pagan
> beings, I saw that PC Lyre's patience was waning. I knew
> I was not helping my case nor demonstrating that I had a
> grip on reality...

Dr Hushson implored Daniel to take his medication. 'What choice did I have?'[13] Daniel writes in his notes. 'I took the medication and washed it down with a glass of pig water[14] provided by the pharmacist.'

Only in hindsight did Daniel realise that the tablet he had been given was larger and more oval in shape than the Lobottymed tablets he had taken previously. As the first waves of dizziness began to overwhelm him, he panicked. Though he did not recall how, he later writes that in his next concrete memory he was:

> ...out-of-breath, wrapped in an Action Man bed sheet,
> running down a town street I didn't know. Two police
> officers grabbed me. I thrashed and squirmed, imploring
> pedestrians to help. They just stared impassively. I was
> taken to the police station, given clothes, and held in an
> interview room. Dr Hushson arrived. He appeared leaner
> than he had done before my 'blackout', and his temples
> were also greyer. He was accompanied by PC Lyre and

[13.] This kind of medical coercion was routine in the 1970s. GPs were well known for imposing unwanted medication regimes on reluctant patients and going to great lengths to do so. Some were known to break into patients' homes, hide in cupboards and wait until dark before sneaking out with hypodermic syringes. Others trained cockroaches or spiders to carry medicine in specially designed rucksacks through patients' noses or mouths into their stomachs while they slept.

[14.] Pig's urine was very popular in the 1970s and was thought to alleviate the squeamishness brought on by drinking pig's urine.

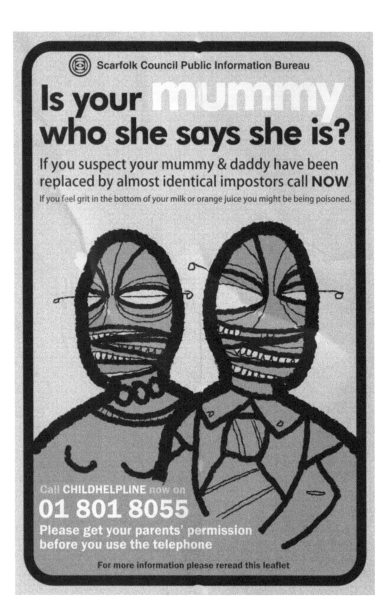

A leaflet warning children about the dangers of parental impostors.[15] As they were in circulation before Daniel's arrival it is possible he may have seen one, or read about one of the familial impostor cases in the newspaper and the concept was subconsciously planted.

a woman called Mrs Payne I'd never met before. All were profusely apologetic. Not only did they acknowledge that I had been right all along, that Joe and Oliver existed, but they told me that my boys had been found alive and well. I couldn't contain my relief and sobbed. A newspaper reporter and photographer were present to capture the moment when I was reunited with my boys...

Daniel's relief was short-lived. Though the boys resembled Joe and Oliver, he insisted that they were not his children.

BIG

I explained that there had been a mistake. Hushson quietly but firmly encouraged me to accept the strange boys. When the boy that was supposed to be Oliver called me daddy and showed me his dinosaur, I lost it. I panicked and bolted ~~plastic dinosaur~~ TOY

I didn't get far. I was overwhelmed by policemen and pinned to the ground. As I struggled, two inexplicable things occurred: firstly, I became aware of a rhythmical 'ker-chack' sound, as if someone was using a large staple gun nearby. Even stranger, out of the corner of my eye, I caught a glimpse of the two boys. The more I looked at them the more it became obvious to me that they were Joe and Oliver. Only a few moments before I'd been 100% sure that the boys were unknown to me. I couldn't explain it.

---

15. The subject of familial imposters in Scarfolk comes up several times in Daniel's archive, and we will return to the subject later. One newspaper article on the subject described how parents were being supplanted by eerie doppelgangers. Only children could spot the subtle differences. For a time, affected children found a gritty substance in their school milk. At first poison was suspected but it turned out to be sand from a beach hundreds of miles away. Despite police investigations none of the impostors were ever positively identified and there was a growing belief in the community that they might not even be human. The impostors vanished as inexplicably as they had arrived when the children's real, bewildered parents were found wandering on the very same beach from which the sand had originated. They had no idea how they had arrived there, how long they had been away or what had happened during their absence.

We may never know how much time transpired between Daniel taking Dr Hushson's unidentified medication and Daniel being confronted with the two boys. Having thoroughly assessed his notes, I believe that he might have been subjected to a regime of systematic brainwashing[16] and drugging, which could have affected his ability to accurately record events.

But why would someone want to do this to him?

At this stage in the unfolding narrative, I consider it crucial to turn our attention to the town of Scarfolk itself. How did the town appear to the outside world, and will we, in its public face, find any expression that offers us an explanation for the events that befell Daniel Bush and his sons?

What follows are several excerpts from Daniel's Scarfolk tourist guide. Though the guide's author or authors are unknown, here we read for the first time the voice of Scarfolk itself – Scarfolk in its own words, if you will.

[16.] Daniel's experiences appear consistent with those described by other people who have been subjected to brainwashing, cognitive conditioning and blow-drying.

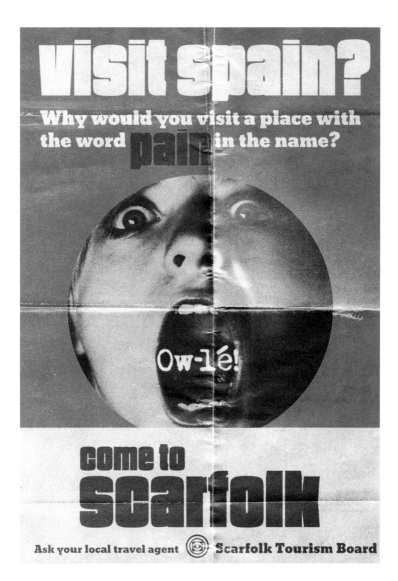

British tourism suffered when Brits began holidaying on the much dirtier Continent in the early 1970s.

a Scarfolk Books book

Discovering Scarfolk

For tourists & other trespassers

With free map* & rabies hand wipes

*map is not of Scarfolk

Introduction

Welcome to Scarfolk in the county of Scarfolkshire. From our rich, fabricated heritage to the complete decimation and modernisation of our historical areas, whether you are wealthy or superfluous, there is something for everyone in Scarfolk.

For the well-to-do, there are boutique shopping arcades selling all manner of homemade craft items, from wooden things and other things to items of varied description.

Then there's the police flea market which sells forensic evidence from unsolved cases. Find yourself a bargain among the confiscated weapons, drug caches and even unclaimed body parts. If you literally have only a few coins in your pocket, do not despair; there are many other towns in Britain willing to tolerate people like you.

Why not visit Scarfolk Ghettown, the city quarter set aside for the working class and other undesirables? Here you can drink and shout all day long, and spend many a long hour completely missing all of life's subtle nuances and simple pleasures for the sake of empty sensual thrills. Try a pint of Ghettown's own Castraspay Neuter Ale, which is specially brewed to sterilise the prolifically reproductive proletariat.

In Ghettown you will also find our war memorial which commemorates those lost or misplaced in the two main wars, as well as the smaller, less interesting ones.

The memorial, which is made from reinforced cardboard, lets visitors pretend that the sacrifice of so many people was for the greater good, and not the outcome of poor decisions made by incompetent, obdurate militarists who believed that imaginary deities endorsed them.

For the more active and adventurous, Scarfolk has dozens of closed mills and factories. Why not indulge your incautious side in an unguided exploration of the many dilapidated buildings? Try your hand at operating the historical machines that maimed and killed hundreds of workers during the region's industrial boom. Get stuck in, but do not get stuck. Try your hand, but don't lose it!

Or maybe you would prefer the clean, fresh air of the Drop. Scarfolk's famous cliffs at 3a Wrake Lane between the post office and Cunttison's Men Swear shop have long been visited by visitors looking for alleviation from life's inevitable disappointments. Scarfolk Drop is not attended by police, Samaritans or social workers and is open more than 7 days a week, 367 days a year. So what are you waiting for? Make room for someone better than you.

Whatever you do during your trip to Scarfolk we hope that you will enjoy your stay and appreciate just how much effort we made to accommodate people like you*.

Your happiness is our concern

*Upon arrival please register with the tourist decontamination centre.

Things to visit

Scarfolk Catgut Mill

Experience for yourself the horrific conditions under which children worked during the Victorian era and see how Scarfolk Council is battling to maintain this traditional attitude to children in the workplace. View the semi-mummified 130-year-old remains of little James Pigeon, only discovered this year, jammed between the lopping-gouge and scraper-sever machines.

James Pigeon stuffed toys are available in the gift shop. Realistic removable fingers. Battering not included.

50p from the sale of every James Pigeon will go towards Gone To The Dogs, the charity that cares for feral children raised by packs of wild Cocker Spaniels.

Open Saturdays and other days.

Old Market Square

You can now take a tour of Scarfolk's historical market square from the comfort of your own car. It is, or rather was, located where the Market View multi-storey car park now stands. The Market Square was originally situated approximately 22 feet below Level 0 between exits 0A and 0B and is commemorated with the sticker attached to the fire extinguisher by the disabled parking spaces.

Open 9am to 9pm.
Good parking facilities.

On Foot Tour

Why not book one of our Scarfolk On Foot tours? The tour is unguided and no maps are provided so that you can make the most of your adventure.

£12.25 per hour. (Shoes not included.)

Scarfolk Council Bunker Tour

(Note: There is a circulating leaflet concerning a vast complex of secret council bunkers that extends for hundreds of miles underground and allegedly contains, among other things, millions of prosthetic eyes and enormous pencil sharpener guillotines. The council bunkers do NOT exist; please do not ask about them.)

Scarfolk Towers Council Estate

Following a spate of serial killings in this infamous, pentangle-shaped high-rise council estate, the surviving residents were moved to new, secure accommodations. However, you and your children can now visit the housing blocks which have been transformed into a themed holiday village.

Stumped police forensics teams will show you around the murder locations that have not yet been cleaned; test your skills of deduction with our dental record comparison game; take a crash course in autopsy forensics. Maybe YOU can work out who the killer is and win a prize of £750!

(Note: You are not eligible for any prize pay-out if you are the killer. Furthermore, any attempt to further tamper with the evidence will impede and confuse the on-going police/tourist investigation.)

Scarfolk Towers

Scarfolk's War Shed

Take a trip down memory lane at Scarfolk's War Shed. Treat yourself and your children to a nostalgic trip to wartime Britain. Relive the moment when you received the news that your father, son or brother was killed overseas.

Visit our field hospital reconstruction and find out why they would not let you see the body.

Free entry to the under-5s and any deceased service men or women.
Free parking (for vehicles only).

Parks and gardens

Scarpark

Why take your kids to a conventional park that is in a constant state of decay? Come instead to Scarfolk's Scarpark, the home of Britain's largest inorganic park.

All trees, flowers and bushes are constructed from the finest, smooth British concrete, as is the children's playground. No more dying foliage, no more randomly clashing natural colours, Scarpark's uniform whiteish-grey shades are soothing to the eye and soul.

Open daily apart from weekends and Mondays to Thursdays.

Bottucks Pond

Set in acres of picturesque fields, miles from the nearest telephone, you will find bottomless Bottucks Pond where many dozens of children have met their ends over the years.

Bring a picnic, take a sedative and doze on the shore while your kids paddle, splash and thrash about and shriek playfully in the weed-tangled waters.

Open nightly.

Bottucks Pond

Outsiders' Zoo & Slaughter Gardens

Unwelcome visitors to Scarfolk are always welcome at Scarfolk's Outsiders' Zoo. Here you will find dozens of open cages and enclosures. Don't be shy – step inside and take a look round.

Why not bring a picnic, games and even some of your most valuable possessions? Please also ensure that your clothing is made only of natural fibres as synthetic fibres pollute the atmosphere when burnt.

ALL sporting events are currently CANCELLED in Scarfolk. For further details please read the council message below:

"The council feels that sports are stylised warfare analogies. This means that they are not proper war. As such, they distract people from the meaning of true, honourable conflict and diminish the role of traditional hostility in modern society.

A few dedicated and gallant people are desperately trying to champion time-honoured violence by introducing it to the football terraces and croquet fields, but, sadly, they are in the minority. There are simply not enough of these selfless souls to make a real difference. Unless we take imitation conflict out of the sports ground and return authentic aggression to the streets and into family homes, we run the risk of losing our national identity, our Britishness.

Britishness was not built on 'pretending' to liberate lesser countries such as India, large swathes of Africa and Wales; it 'actually' liberated them. And it did not use shuttle cocks and rubber balls to do it; it used swords and guns. Whoever heard of a successful massacre being carried out by ski jumpers or synchronised swimmers? Would Britain have won the war in the desert if, instead of tanks, it had deployed toboggans? An intercontinental ballistic thermo nuclear missile cannot be averted by even the most skilled trampolinist.

Scarfolk stadium will be converted into gladiator training school for the under 10s.

If we let ourselves get excited when a snooker player pots a ball or a footballer scores a goal we may forget the simple traditional thrills of jabbing an enemy with a biro or kicking someone's head over a fence. If that happens we do not win; we score an own goal.

Say no to pseudo war. And make peace with your true, violent heritage.

If you feel as strongly as we do about the damaging influence of sports in society, why not join Scarfolk's Real Aggro or Thump Chums clubs? They meet every Thursday evening at St Sorrowfetish church where you will find yourself among like-minded friends. Maybe you would even like to join our society's five-a-side team."

Places to stay

Snoopend Cottage

Rooms and suites available. All private. No surveillance whatsoever.
None of the rooms are bugged or filmed from behind two-way mirrors. Doors on most rooms. Breakfasts contain only normal food, no sodium pentothal.
If you would like a complete recording of your stay just ask at reception.

Bell End View Hotel

Conveniently located close to the outside.
Non-yelping disabled people welcome. (Disabled rooms available on the 10th floor. No lift, but exterior rope pulley system available.)
Vegetarians welcome to find alternative accommodation.
Telephone: 0310986981

B&B #34B/1

Located in the centre of Scarfolk's outskirts.
12 hirsute rooms.
Some rooms contain TVs (w/GSOH).
Foreigners welcome if accompanied by legal guardians/owners.
Ground floor access to all floors.
Breakfast served 4am-4.04am.
Telephone: 0310986991

Happy Welcome Inn

Dozens of partially-clean rooms always available.
No children, babies, pets, blacks, homosexuals, Jews, left-wingers/liberals, Irish, unionists, ginger-haireds, or Eurovision contestants. See our pamphlet for the full exclusion list.
English breakfast only (no continental).

Jan & Mike's B&B&Q

Jan and Mike have run their bed, breakfast & quarantine hostel for 5 years.
Isolation rooms with TV, kettle and real leather restraints.
Free catheters for the over-10s.
Incontinent and full English breakfast available.
Free tea and coffee for any residents suffering from accidental contagion

Snoopend Cottage

Getting about

Scarfolk is well served by buses, taxis and a unique underground train system which was originally an overground train system built on unstable land.

For buses please go to the bus station. For trains please go to the bus station where you will be able to get a bus to the train station.

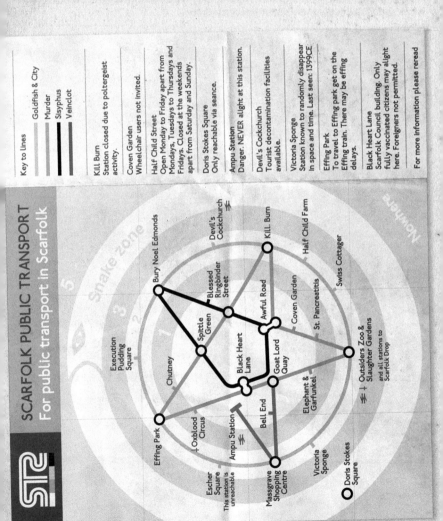

Key to lines

— Goldfish & City
— Murder
— Sisyphus
— Velnclot

Kill Burn
Station closed due to poltergeist activity.

Coven Garden
Wheelchair users not invited.

Half Child Street
Open Monday to Friday apart from Mondays, Tuesdays to Thursdays and Fridays. Closed at the weekends apart from Saturday and Sunday.

Doris Stokes Square
Only reachable via seance.

Ampu Station
Danger. NEVER alight at this station.

Devil's Cockchurch
Tourist decontamination facilities available.

Victoria Sponge
Station known to randomly disappear in space and time. Last seen: 1399CE

Effing Park
To travel to Effing park get on the Effing train. There may be effing delays.

Black Heart Lane
Scarfolk Council building. Only fully vaccinated citizens may alight here. Foreigners not permitted.

For more information please reread

SCARFOLK PUBLIC TRANSPORT
For public transport in Scarfolk

A postcard for Scarfolk Drop, which was popular among despondent visitors.

A tourism poster for Scarfolk Drop.[17]

In addition to the tourist guide there are several pages from limited-run publications written by local historians, such as Andrew Flem, a renowned, supernatural pornographer.

The first excerpt is from a book about the Scarfolk Council building. It is followed by an excerpt from a publication about local legends and folklore called *Stories of Olde Scarfolke.*

[17.] Targeting depressives and the terminally ill, the tourism & leisure board exaggerated how exciting Scarfolk's attractions were. They banked on the inevitable disappointment of already despondent tourists and hoped they would hurl themselves from Scarfolk Drop. Scarfolk children would comb the beaches for washed-up snow globes, key-rings, tea towels and other items which were then resold in the gift shop - an early example of recycling.

Chapter 2

The History of the Council Building

Scarfolk Town Hall, which now houses the town council, was partially rebuilt in 1970 following a mysterious fire. Tragically, all members of the council perished apart from Mayor Ritter who had only just been inaugurated that week. By his own admission, he was lucky to have survived the blaze. By chance, he had been trying out an all-in-one flame

A mental photograph taken by a 17th century seer who prophesised the Scarfolk Town Hall fire in 1684.

resistant suit when the flames took hold. Unfortunately, he did not have time to warn his colleagues.

Freelance occultist and architect Ken Nightbrook worked on the reconstruction of the building, which had not always served as a town hall. It was a hospital for over two hundred years and known by various names: St Cacoethes; St Jeff's; the Scarfolk Hospital for Disgusting Pariahs; Dr Eddie's Mental Basket and Tearooms; The Clinic for Possessed Berserkers of the Nameless Lord.

Around the 8th century there was a temple on the site. It was worshipped by a cult, the members of which were descended from or neighbours of Neolithic peoples, and to date a large sacred standing stone, covered with incomprehensible symbols, still dominates the foyer of the building. Legend says that anyone who touches the stone will shortly thereafter receive a complimentary selection of office equipment, as lay office worker Annie Byrne could have testified. In May 1904, mere hours after polishing the stone, she was found by colleagues writhing on the floor of her office, covered with large, pinching bulldog clips. Not a single inch of bare flesh was visible and it took her colleagues several hours to free her from the unyielding, black metal jaws.

It is tales such as these that may have inspired the ghostly stories of the 1930s. No sooner had the building been converted to the town's new council office than it had to close because of poltergeist activity, which, back then, was officially reported as 'episodes of unstationary stationery'. Workers were rained on with ghostly paper; typewriter ribbon would, like living vines, strangle people; post room boys would find themselves stapled to noticeboards and typewriters would suddenly fly off desks or type out mysterious cheques payable to the mayor. Even the office canteen was affected and employees would frequently find themselves fleeing from flying cutlery, showers of boiling soup and demented sandwiches.

A sketch that captures alleged poltergeist activity, which started again in the 1970s. A TV (top right) floats around the office.

Overleaf, a secretary fends off an attack by a cinnamon teacake that claimed to be possessed by the spirit of a Victorian convict called Arthur Hands who hated cinnamon teacakes during his lifetime and much preferred scones.

The Silent Spirit

Scarfolk's Excellentil Hotel (now Scarfolk's book burning facility) was haunted by a ghost known locally as The Silent Spirit which was renowned for its considerate nature and the fact that it had never been seen or heard. Spookily, it never left any sign of its existence whatsoever, which baffled ghost-hunters for decades.

An artist's impression of The Silent Spirit

Jesus

A legend tells of the time that Jesus travelled to Scarfolk to attend a carpentry conference in nearby Blackstock. By all accounts there was an argument about the robustness of different hinge-joints and Jesus was ejected from the conference, to great applause, by Ken Trumberts, the keynote speaker, who resented having his expertise questioned by a 'self-righteous foreigner'. Ironically, the wooden brace that Trumberts invented to support his wife's washing line was adapted by the Romans to hold crucifixes in place. Previously, they had been very unsafe and were always toppling over, causing unnecessary injuries to the person being crucified. Trumbert became so renowned for his safety device that in the 1st century AD crucifixion victims even acquired the nickname 'Mrs T's Bloomers'.

Slap Tuesday [18]

Once a year in Scarfolk the townspeople gather to slap a minor celebrity. This originates in an ancient ritual during which an animal was whipped annually to expiate the sins of the community. In 1632 no animals were available because they were all being tried for witchcraft and attempting to set up an illegal distillery below Scarfolk church. The community had to use a pantomime horse instead. Over the years this concept broadened to include any stage and, subsequently, film and TV actors. The sin aspect was also transferred and to this day many people still believe that out-of-work celebrities are bad luck and will not let them in their homes.

[18.] For more about annual customs in Scarfolk see page 100.

The Chihenkin

The Chihenkin is a beast from local folklore. It is said to be a chicken possessed by the spirit of a hen. Over the years, many thousands of fowl have been slaughtered by unnerved farmers desperate to eliminate the Chihenkin, but it always avoids detection by perfectly imitating a chicken that just happens to be visiting from a nearby farm. Legend says that if you eat an egg laid by a Chihenkin you will invent something that benefits mankind in the short term, but in the long term it will destroy the world. In 1850 Jonathan George invented the knee-length sock after eating what he believed was a Chihenkin's egg. So convinced was he that his invention could bring about the demise of humanity that he threw himself, along with his original, highly-detailed sock blueprints, into the path of a speeding train. Back then trains only went about 35mph so George survived. However, his legs were severed... just below the knee. The severed stumps were preserved, complete with socks and are on display in Scarfolk Museum, where they patiently await their opportunity to destroy the world.

the fearsome chihenkin

The mythological Chihenkin. From a 13th century illuminated manuscript photocopied by an order of Cistern monks.

Scarfolk Henge

It is said that the Devil herself built the Neolithic henge just outside Scarfolk. For many years, locals were not really sure what Scarfolk's pretentiously arranged wooden stumps represented. Some believed that they were intended as some sort of construction, others insisted that they form a kind of shape. Medieval scholars were convinced that it was designed as a calendar to remind primitive peoples of important dates such as Christmas, school holidays and dental visits. However, researchers today believe that the building project was not completed due to lack of finances. The henge is actually the framework for an incomplete multi-storey parking area for carts and horses.

The Coprofilly Fairies

In 1900 two Scarfolk girls took photographs of what they claimed were fairies at the bottom of their garden at Coprofilly House. Britain was soon buzzing with talk of the fairies, especially when the girls managed to capture one of the supernatural beings, which they sent to the Zoological Society of London. Frustratingly for the society's research members, the fairy cadaver must have somehow magically transformed into papier-mâché during transit. Many people blamed the post office and demanded that the managing director be charged with gnomicide. However, society members visited the girls' home and found that the fairies appeared to turn to papier-mâché the moment human eyes made contact with them. When the girls died of glue poisoning a few years later, the fairies stopped appearing and locals believe this is because they were so saddened by the deaths of the girls.

The Scarfolk Beast

There was a car accident on Scarfolk Moors in November 1975. The driver veered off the road after being distracted by a dark, hulking entity stalking across the barren, misty landscape. The driver tried to film the entity with his Super8 film camera, but the footage has since been lost.

Many believe this was a confirmed sighting of the Scarfolk Beast, which was spotted around town for many years. Though many townspeople claim to have seen the Beast, descriptions vary: 'It had the head and upper body of a fish and the lower body of a mermaid'; 'it looked like a child salesman glued to a shag-pile carpet'; 'it looked a bit like a horned bear carrying what looked like a briefcase. It seemed to be heading in the direction of the bus stop.'

The Coprofilly girls, Bernard and Spud (and Spud's inexplicable growth. which everybody called Nelson).

Daniel was particularly interested in the Scarfolk Beast, which he believed might offer some explanation for the figure that had been present at his wife's death and whose presence was suggested at the disappearance of his sons in the form of staples and hole-punch paper. What follows is a cover from *The Unexplaineded*, a now defunct monthly magazine that addressed topics that were 'unexplaindable', as well as photographs taken by Scarfolk residents of the so-called Beast. Despite mounting evidence and calls from the public to investigate, the council declined to launch an official inquiry into the phenomenon.

50pea

THE
Unexplaineded
MYSTERIES & OTHER UNINFORMED SPECULATIO₁

Poltergeists & unstationary stationery
Identified flying objects
Stigmata of the dump
Supernatural fudge
The Scarfolk Beast

7

® Aus & NZ $1.75 IR 85p US$1.5

This diversion into Scarfolk has given us a deeper insight into the 'personality' of the town, if that is the right word. The tourist guide not only gives us a better understanding of Daniel's predicament at the time, but also, more importantly, it becomes an anchor in an increasingly chaotic, unsettling body of evidence and prepares us for what happened to him next.

A chance shot of the Scarfolk Beast? The image also contains a flying object which was later identified as an unidentified flying object.

Opposite: Issue 7 of The Unexplaineded *magazine which tried to explain the unexplainedable but only rarely offered tangible explanations, leaving most unexplainedable phenomena unexplained. Pictured is the Neolithic hill figure on Scarfolk Mound that some believe depicts the Scarfolk Beast. The figure appears to hold a staple gun in its hand. The phallus resembles a paperclip.*

The photographer claimed to have caught this image of the Scarfolk Beast (to the right, behind the man's head). However, sceptics insist that the mysterious object may simply be a prehistoric seagull caught in a time slip.

This photograph captures what appears to be the Scarfolk Beast taking a stroll on Scarfolk Common in 1977.

FIRM STOOLS! SOFT STOOLS!

ALL HIGH FIBRE!

While stocks last

Don't let your behind fall behind. At the SFS summer sale you will find all the latest fashions in indolence.

Our Product Promise to you: If it is a stool you want, we will ensure that is exactly what you get. Guaranteed.

Scarfolk Furniture Stores **SFS**

Open Bank Holiday Monday.
Closed during police raids

We're a shop!

This 1979 magazine advertisement for Scarfolk Furniture Stores seems innocent enough. But Daniel noticed a figure that should not have been there (top right).

Throughout the 1970s, Staples cereal was a staple cereal. Daniel believed that the brand's cartoon mascot was the Scarfolk Beast, though he could never prove it.

The 'Missing Years'

THIS SECTION OF the archive is not only much more fragmented, less linear in nature, but it is also highly personal. It deals with what Daniel called his 'Missing Years'. What transpired during this period is a question Daniel asked himself a thousand times. His sole focus seems to have been trawling his memory for even the vaguest, dimmest recollections.

Daniel's 'Missing Years' began on the floor of the police station as he stared into the eyes of the two children he at first claimed were impostors, a claim he abruptly, inexplicably retracted. Daniel's subsequent actions seem to defy reason.

He did not leave Scarfolk to continue on his journey to Sedaton[19] as planned. Instead, he and his alleged sons moved into a small three-storey bungalow in Scarfolk. Astonishingly, according to Daniel's notes, 'I'm not entirely sure how long I lived there. It was an impenetrable haze; it could have been years before I was liberated from my imposed stupefaction.'[20]

[19.] According to my research, the house that Daniel had bought there lay empty for years until, quite coincidentally, the Sedaton council requisitioned it and converted it into a safe house for vulnerable parents who had reported their abusive children to the authorities. *(See p. 59.)*

[20.] 'Imposed stupefaction' is not to be confused with 'voluntary indifference'. Teenagers in the 1970s, disillusioned by rising unemployment figures, objected to factual subjects being taught in the schools. They wanted to do away with Maths, English and Geography and replace them with subjects such as 'advanced rolling around on the floor' and 'food sentiency' (some scientists believed that if we could communicate with food it would save us having to go all the way to the kitchen: we could just shout at it and order it about).

The nature of Daniel's disjointed recollections support my theory that he was being drugged and brainwashed. Perhaps most disturbingly, as time wore on, Daniel's mind was reduced to that of an infant or gym teacher.

He was visited daily, at the behest of Dr Hushson, by Mrs Payne, a dowdy, local primary school teacher in her early forties. She fed, bathed and clothed him and his perception of her became distorted over time. 'I began thinking of her as my mother and even called her "mummy" on several occasions. It was the same with Dr Hushson, whom I called "daddy-medicine". My relationship to "Joe and Oliver" also warped. I wasn't sure if they were my sons or twin brothers.'

Daniel's earliest memories of this period were largely domestic. He was never allowed to leave the bungalow, so his recollections of it are invaluable: 'It could have had 3 rooms or 300. I didn't know if I was in a bedroom or living room, if the lights were on or off, or even if I was alone or in company.'

I have only very loosely drawn together Daniel's artefacts and memory fragments by subject: consumables; household and pharmaceutical products; magazines; television images; board games; LPs and tapes – the quotidian ephemera of a life. And my commentary serves only to widen the reader's understanding of the environment in which Daniel found himself.

NEVER
GO WITH
STRANGE
CHILDREN

Never accept sweets, cigarettes or alcohol from a child.

Never accept a lift from a child or go with him on his tricycle.

If a child offers to show you some race horses, flies or leopards firmly say "no."

Children carry more than 72 known diseases. A bite or scratch can be fatal.

Children have paranormal abilities and can wreak havoc in the lives of unsuspecting grown-ups.

IF YOU SEE A SUSPICIOUS CHILD
REPORT IT IMMEDIATELY
TO YOUR LOCAL COVEN OR LYNCH MOB

**Grown-ups
Protection
GuPS Society**

For more information please reread this poster

A council poster warning vulnerable adults about predatory children. Adult abuse was a nationwide problem.

Household Products

Daniel had memories of being fed foods with very high sugar content, which at the time he took to be treats, but in retrospect realised that, like his medications, they were all part of a finely tuned process to strictly regulate his sleep and waking patterns.

Expiry Dates.[21] *A popular confectionary in the 1970s. Daniel scribbled 'remember this' on the back of this wrapper, but did not specify what it was he was supposed to recall. He wrote many such cryptic messages on the backs of sweet wrappers, receipts, etc., most likely to avoid detection.*

Opposite, bottom: A Coloured Berry Jam label. Many consumers were uncomfortable when this jam arrived on the shelves from overseas. They claimed it was taking the jobs that would have normally gone to English jams. Ultimately, they told Scarco to send the jam back to where it came from.

[21.] In 1978 children all over Scarfolk fell ill and developed malignant sores on their mittens. The culprit was found to be a chocolate and dried date bar called Expiry Dates. The confectionary was found to contain only .05g of actual edible foodstuffs, while the lion's share of ingredients included various ominous-sounding toxins, building site debris and part of a discarded pram. Even the dates were found to be reconstituted beetle exoskeletons. To make amends, the manufacturers created a new chocolate bar called Chemowhizz which contained chemotherapeutic agents. The idea was to treat the sick children while also maintaining more important company sales targets. Unfortunately, though the children survived, the ingredients were imbalanced, triggering other side-effects such as the development of husky Scottish accents.

Above: Wagon Weevils. The product was eventually withdrawn when the weevils were found not to be members of the National Union of Ingredients.

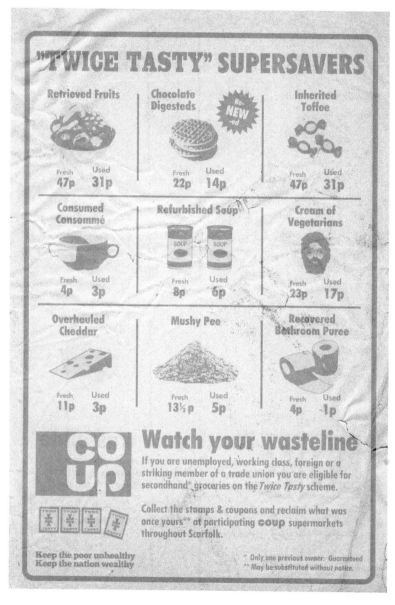

The Co-Up's reusable food scheme to aid the poor and other social disappointments.

An E-Cola bottle label. The brand's proud slogan was 'A different bacterium in every bubble or there'll be trouble!'

Unsolicited Meat. When the product was tested by food scientists it was found to contain human DNA. For a time, this lead to Unsolicited Meat being given the right to vote.

Owls were believed to be a wonder food. However, when consumers became wiser after eating owl they realised that this was not the case after all.

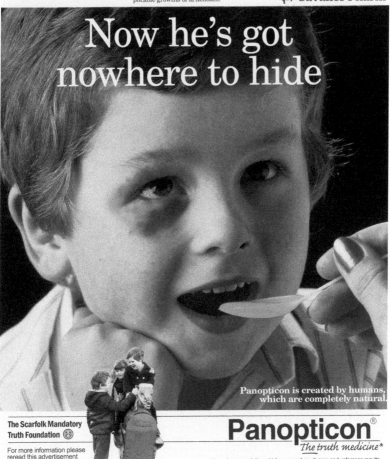

Kills 99% of
KNOWN LIES
but only 3% of children

Uses: For relief from personal freedom and the pain of autonomy.

Prescribing information: Each 5ml contains 5ml of medicine. No lumps of fat or gristle guaranteed.

Dose: 950ml 24 times daily.

Side effects: Allergic reactions include mild nausea, death-like symptoms, inexplicable growths of artichokes.

Panopticon triggers a chemically induced psychosis which induces a split personality in the child.

One of these personalities can be subsequently controlled and employed as an informant against the other half.

Ⓟ Cavalier Pharm

Now he's got
nowhere to hide

Panopticon is created by humans,
which are completely natural.

**The Scarfolk Mandatory
Truth Foundation** Ⓢ

For more information please
reread this advertisement

Panopticon®
*The truth medicine**

* based on speculation which may produce diverse and unforseen results.

A 1978 advertisement for the truth drug Panopticon. The advertising agency prohibited its copywriters from using the drug while they worked on the campaign.

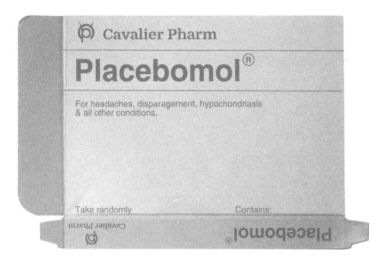

According to the packet, the only side-effect of Placebomol tablets was 'Inevitably dying of the genuine condition you took the tablets for in the first place.'

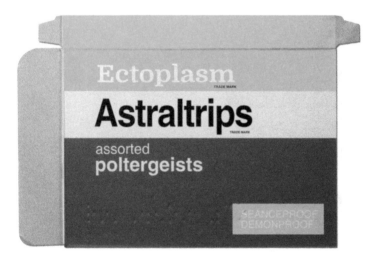

If a person's mobility was limited after an accident, poltergeists were used to run errands.

Books

Mrs Payne frequently read children's books to Daniel, Joe and Oliver each evening as they slipped into a medication-induced haze. Daniel wrote that he 'found some of the words difficult', which supports the idea that his mental capacity was diminished. 'It was as though my personality were being erased and then reprogrammed to assimilate me into the Scarfolk way of doing things.'

An important facet of assimilation meant being indoctrinated against people and groups deemed to be 'outsiders', or 'Scarfnots', as they were known. Non-Caucasians for sure, but also residents who had inadvertently developed the semblance of a tan. Those who lived more than a mile outside of Scarfolk did not escape being branded as outsiders and even migrating birds and animals were not trusted.

Handicapped & Disabled Jokes, *Penguin, 1976. Disabled people also often found themselves branded as outsiders and were the butt of myriad jokes. However, in the late 1970s the legal definition of disability was widened to include anyone who was not born by immaculate conception.*

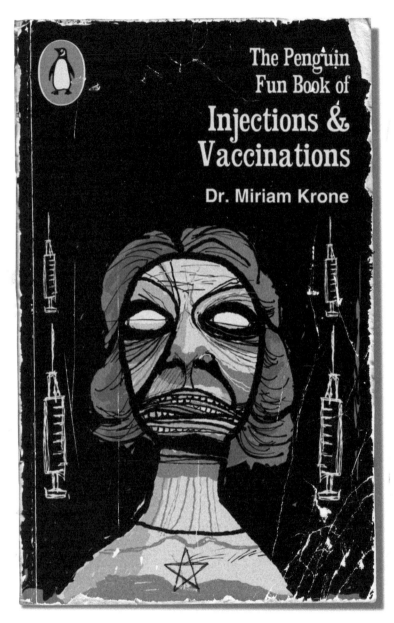

Injections & Vaccinations, *Penguin, 1973. This was a very popular book among children, as were hypodermic needles. Shops were always sold out well in advance of Christmas.*

Paranoia about foreigners and outsiders, most of whom it was believed were taught from an early age to worship demons and how to kill, was rife and until 1978 foreigners were officially classified by the government as livestock and subcategorised by odour.

Defining who was and was not English became complicated. By the end of the decade, right-wing nationalists had drawn up a list demanding the deportation of everyone apart from nine people, all of who claimed to be the only true English. They even insisted on the deportation of all foreign foods (which they later amended, granting special visas to pizza, kebab and curry sauce).

Their spokesperson, Colin Head, the brother-in-law of PC Lyre, said at a 1976 rally:

> **"We REJECT all foreign influences in England.**
> That is our weltanschauung.
> Multiculturalism is our bête noire and we strongly believe that English culture is destined to become kaput if the current zeitgeist continues to be de rigueur. But it doesn't have to be a fait accompli and that's why we will continue to be the enfant terrible of modern politics.
> It's time to act: Carpe Diem!"

COLIN HEAD

Little White Sam, *Scarfolk Books, Repr. 1970, was withdrawn because the pale-skinned figure reminded children from developing countries of brutal days under British and European rule. This was a major blow because, historically, white people felt they had always been unfairly picked on for trying to help the world be more like them and Jesus. To avoid contentious material regarding race, colour and gender, the later reprinted edition re-imagined Sam as a transparent, asexual flatworm.*

Foreigners & How to Spot Them: Safe Methods of Approach, *Penguin, 1973.*

Institutionalised racism was rife. On the surface, the message of this allegedly innocuous British Rail poster is one that deals with the dangers of using dark magic to animate giant demon toys, following the case of schoolboy Peter Colons who brought to life an immense Slinky that killed 237 people and destroyed public property. The council denied any subliminal bigotry and when racism was finally exposed as being detrimental to society, it was blamed on foreigners.

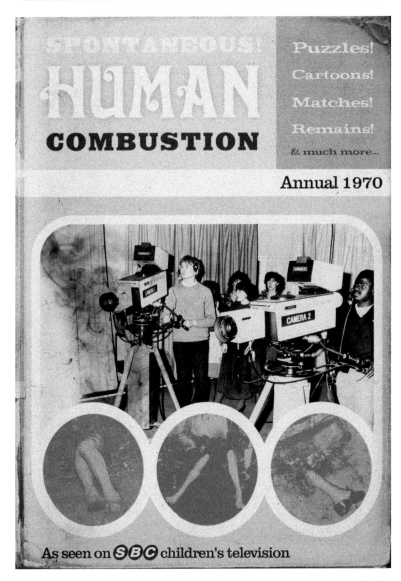

Spontaneous! Human Combustion Annual, *SBC Books, 1970. Based on the after-school children's light-entertainment TV programme of the same name. The programme's victims or rather contestants were frequently not of British descent, or even Scarfolk descent. It ran for only one series and sparked a catchphrase still occasionally heard today: 'Douse the louse, Mr Chrysanthemum!' – the name of the show's host.*

But not all of Daniel's books touch on themes of race. Another television annual cover in Daniel's archive is *Dentistry for the Deceased*, which accompanied a live Saturday night programme that was enjoyed by all the family.

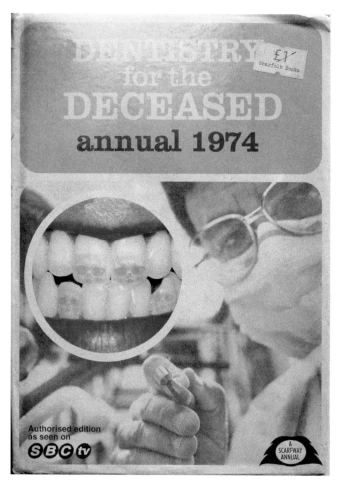

Dentistry for the Deceased Annual, *SBC Books, 1974. During the programme, dead celebrities were paired with living dentists who created spectacular and exciting post-mortem smiles against the clock.*

Television

Television was compulsory in Scarfolk and some programmes, particularly those about local government, had to be watched dozens of times consecutively. *We Watch You Watching Us*, for example, shown every Sunday evening, was a 6-hour surveillance programme made by the Scarfolk Broadcasting Corporation and only broadcast locally. In addition to uncensored surveillance recordings of Scarfolk residents, it included celebrity interrogations, dance routines with striking miners in swimwear, and a situation comedy called *Malcolm & Mary*, which featured Christian activists Malcolm Whitehouse and Mary Muggeridge running a faith-friendly sex shop that sold items such as anal prayer beads. The programme was made by the same production company responsible for *Song of Prayer*, *Praise for the Day* and other programmes with totalitarian themes. Daniel later noted that he believed the programme theme tune, like many of time period, was composed specifically to induce viewers into a suggestible, hypnotic state.

We Watch You Watching Us, *SBC TV continuity screen, 1970s.*

Schools & Colleges daytime programming covered the spectrum of rudimentary education: Maths, English, Hauntology and Mind Control.

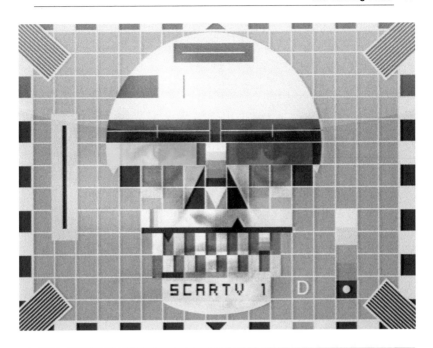

Scarfolk TV test cards. It was illegal to turn off the television while they were being broadcast. As with television programme theme tunes, many believed that the test cards contained subliminal images and sounds.

SATURDAY

6.50   The Playschool Riots
7.20   The Lowest Common De-
        -nominator Family Show
8.10   The Degeneration Game
9.00   News, Weather & Laments
9.25   Film: Viruses Like You
11.00   Mandatory Chants
12.00   Closedown

Details in *Radio Tomes*

Radio Tomes, *a TV, radio and numbers stations listings magazine, 11-17 June 1977.*

Music

Daniel wrote that records and cassettes were also very important to him during his time in the bungalow and while the vast majority of commercial releases were of surveillance recordings, he also listened to and enjoyed music.

In addition to music by internationally loved artists such as Elton John, The Carpenters and Idi Amin, he also listened to albums by local stars, such as Scarfolk's own Fictional Buttocks,[22] and the studio recording of Bill Chunt's hit musical, *Factory-Related Injuries & Deaths*.

Songs about wool scraping, workplace accidents and desirable viruses were very popular in the 1970s. Bill Chunt's pop-up book Factory-Related Injuries & Deaths *was turned into a successful musical in 1976. Scarfolk Records and Tapes.*

[22.] The art-rock group Fictional Buttocks had no human members. It was comprised of one thousand snakes stuffed into an overstretched pair of ladies' tights, and left to squirm clumsily around a fully equipped recording studio.

Illicit Recordings of You & Your Neighbours, *SBC Cassettes, 1973.*

Space Minstrel *by Beige, Scarfolk Records and Tapes, 1977. The album was by far the most successful minstrel-based concept album in rock history.*

Another popular local act was Prog[23] group Beige. *Space Minstrel*, a concept album about a black-and-white minstrel who is accidentally caught in a cosmic apocalypse, featured songs with titles such as 'The Majestic Cosmos of the Infinity-sized Steamboat Vortex and Celestial Dixie Suicide in Top Hat & Tails'. What follows is an excerpt from the sleeve notes that Daniel made a point of highlighting. The reference to 'planet Redtape' is particularly pertinent to his later, crucial investigation of a cult.[24]

> The Earth has been completely smashed up by a rubbish nuclear war. The only survivor, a minstrel, clings to a big lump of rock and hurtles through the spacious universe. He sings show tunes and music-hall favourites to planets such as Redtape as he passes them […] 400 billion years and 3 days later, the minstrel's vocal vibrations are picked up by an alien race who discover a bit of thumb in a white glove. They rebuild him and create millions of copies. The minstrels are given their own planet where they happily sing for what is left of eternity...

[23.] 'Prog' is an abbreviation of 'prognosis', named after a group of stammer-suffering GPs found it easier to sing diagnoses to their patients. The group even released a charity single called 'S-s-s-ix Months to L-l-l-ive (S-s-sorry)'.

[24.] Go to page 106 of this volume for further information.

Games

Music, books and television were not the only forms of entertainment available to Daniel. Whether it was charades, Milgram's Electrocution Game, Drunk Junior Surgeon or Hide and Weep, Daniel recalled playing many games in the bungalow with his sons/brothers. A favourite was Top Tramps – themed packs of cards that rated various objects and people, such as speedboats, motorbikes, prostitutes and, in this case, tramps.

Educational gifts were also very popular among Scarfolk children: chemistry and electronic sets; microscopes and family waterboarding kits sold in their hundreds around Christmas and St Succubus's Day, but the game that Daniel recalled most clearly was the Junior Taxidermy Kit made by Scarfolk Games. It came with a complete set of taxidermist tools downsized for smaller hands: fleshing and filleting knives; skeletal bone cleaner; muscle tissue tissues; weasel stretcher; bum glue and monkey egg flannel. Early editions came with a free humpback whale on which children could practise their burgeoning skills (a whale garrotte was included), though later editions did not include the aquatic mammal.[25]

[25.] Daniel writes that, years later, one of the humpback whale editions was sold in auction for the record price of £499,000 (which is approximately five-hundred thousand pounds in today's money) simply because it is very hard to find the humpback whale edition still in the original packaging.

Top Tramps by Scarfolk Games.

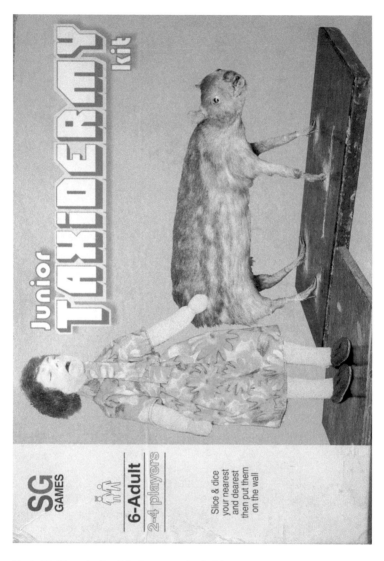

Junior Taxidermy by Scarfolk Games, standard edition.

Super Video Pastime games console, 1979. The computer player developed emotions over time. It became a sore loser, cheated and sometimes even refused to play unless you let it win.

Not all of Daniel's memories were quite so domestic; he also had disquieting recollections of his time in the bungalow. One such memory he describes as a recurring dream that he often had after Dr Hushson medicated and anaesthetised him before bedtime.

I'm standing before a dark tunnel. I'm afraid to go in. There's someone or something lurking in there – an old gypsy woman.[26] She holds up three fingers. Suddenly, she's gone and in her place is a large, muscular creature: dirty, covered with hair. Paperclips and staples flood out of it and stream like a thick swarm of insects toward my face. I can't move my hands as the paperclips fill my nose and mouth. I'm choking, overwhelmed by guilt for all the office supplies I have ever treated carelessly: lost pencils, chewed biros, staples bent out of shape. I scream, vowing to be more respectful and never to misuse a paperclip ever again. That's when I wake up, left with the feeling that I've been posed a riddle to solve. [27]

[26.] I am reminded of Old Hag Syndrome – a hallucinatory state that can occur during the transition from sleep to wakefulness. Sufferers often report seeing an old woman in their bedroom. In 1971 the so-called 'hag' was spotted shopping in Asda. She claimed she had no idea how or why she had suddenly appeared in so many people's homes, but it was very inconvenient, especially because of the cost of getting home on public transport afterwards.

[27.] Fictional and mythological characters have always posed riddles. In English folklore Merlin the magician once set King Arthur a riddle about two dragons and a conker. For many years King Arthur, already an avid gamer, became obsessed with solving the puzzle, which vexed Guinevere and perhaps precipitated her tryst with Lancelot who preferred lawn games and badminton. Before Arthur died he begged Merlin to give him the riddle's answer, but Merlin had completely forgotten about it and suggested that he probably made it up during an odd mood. To this day, in some areas of northern England, unsolvable problems are sometimes called 'Warlocks' bollocks'.

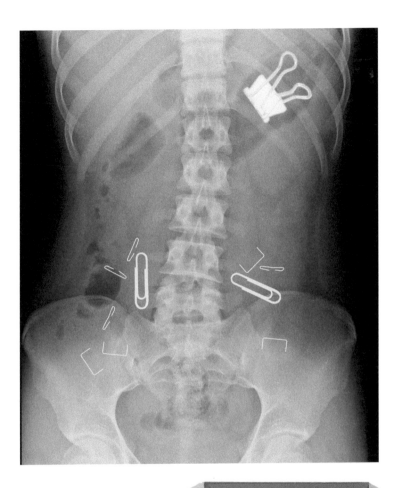

Above: Daniel's notes do not describe how he came by this X-ray, though the patient was probably either male or female. Were Daniel's dreams partly true? Was he being operated on by Dr Hushson and gradually being filled with office supplies?

Right: Festive Paperclips were sold mainly to hospitals, but the public bought packs in their thousands around religious holidays.

100 paperclips for religious use.
To be ingested.

Scarfolk ice-cream

Two words spell ice-cream!

new

old

Soap Virus 8p

Asbest-o-creme 10p

Bulimic Pork Nun 8p

Caramel Rabies Saturdae 8p

Benson & Hedges' Roach Hair 8p

Gammon Bedsore 8p

Vodka Orange 18p
(vol. 40%)

Jesus Fudge Helmet 10p

Fizzy Foreigner 8p

All-the-way-in 10p

Vanilla Pol Pot 8p

Winking Bidet Owl 10p

 old

Honeycomb Glaucoma 8p

Crowley's Evil Goldfish 9p

 new

Milk Gristle 7p

Coconut Chemo 7p
Tomato Chemo 7p

Biopsy Popsy 8p

The Black & White "10p" Lolly 11p

Blue Bottle Flies Eyes Ice 11p

In another of Daniel's barely remembered scenarios, he is at the centre of a circle of people in the bungalow's breakfast room-cum-kitchenette:

> I'm lying face-down on a cold slab, naked apart from
> Womble socks. There's an intense, bright light beneath
> me. It starts at my feet and slowly works its way up my
> body. A pitiful whine accompanies the light. The circle
> chants louder as the unearthly glow creeps toward my
> head. Joe and Oliver [or whoever the boys are] watch on,
> expressionless. I call out to them but they don't respond.
> I can't move. The light reaches my eyes, it's blinding me...
> Now I realise what's happening: I'm on an enormous
> photocopier machine. My expression of horror is captured
> on ream upon ream of paper disgorged by the machine;
> my terrified eyes forever frozen in grainy black and white.
> This happened almost identically many times, though I
> wasn't always wearing Womble socks.

After a lengthy but unknown period in the bungalow, whoever was doing the brainwashing – if indeed that is what was happening – must have felt that Daniel had been broken enough to let him venture outside; however, his memories do not become any clearer. He recalls going shopping with his sons/brothers and mother/carer; flashes of seemingly happy days out; laughing and playing with Joe and Oliver in a concrete park (Daniel writes that all the roundabouts and climbing frames, etc., were in the shape of arcane mystical symbols); going on bike rides; eating ice creams from the van that trundled regularly around Scarfolk's streets.[28]

[28.] From Daniel's notes: 'The ice-cream van man came between 3 & 4 a.m. His van blared out the haunting Swedish Rhapsody numbers station. The ice-cream van man wore a clown mask to disguise the horrific burns on his face because he didn't want to frighten the children. It didn't work. He used clothes pegs to hold the mask on because he was missing an ear. He lived in a nondescript building in an electrical substation and no one knew his name.'

Not all memories were so vague. Daniel clearly recalls attending a school with Joe and Oliver, who he sometimes mistakes for school friends. He claims to have attended the school many times, if not daily and if not daily then at all other times. Despite this, his later investigations into the school yielded no results. Officially at least, it simply did not exist.

The classroom was laid out like any other. Children's crayon sketches on a long-pig, vellum-lined wall. There were rows of pegs, each holding a pupil's coat and chain. I was too big for my chair and flip-top desk.

I realise now that the classroom had no windows, the door was padlocked and it hummed slightly (it was electrified like one of those cow fences) and there were several cameras positioned to capture the room from every angle. Written in big letters above the blackboard was the phrase, 'School days are the happiest days of your life. This is not optional.'

Another thing I also realised much later was that the playground 'outside' was actually a vast hangar-like interior and the sounds of birds, aeroplanes, weather and even children happily playing were played on a loop through a PA system. We played games like Rodeo Monkey, which involved sellotaping a child to a rabid orangutan, which is provoked until it is runs amok. I think it was an orangutan; it might have been a different kind of ape, a hairy child, or even a possessed toy.

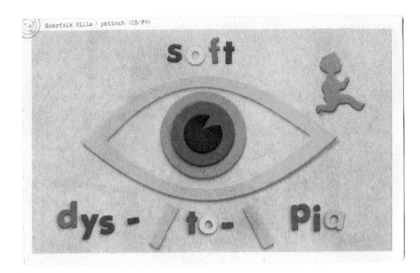

Soft Dystopia. Daniel did not remember how he came by this image.

Daniel offers some corroborative evidence for the existence of the school. He claimed that, on his forearm, he had what looked like a faded birthmark that had not appeared until his first visit to Scarfolk. He claimed that all children had such tattoos which formed series of numbers.[29]

Daniel writes in his notes that, during his later investigations, he could not locate an 'indoor' school in Scarfolk, though he does include the following pages from school textbooks, which he found in a sale of second hand books at Scarfolk library. He believes these books were once taught at this 'secret school'.

[29.] Daniel's was 018118055. This number once was the telephone number of a popular children's television programme called *Exchange Emporium*. According to Daniel's notes, from 1970 it was also the unlisted number of an office in the Scarfolk Council building, though this may be coincidental.

Female reproduction in females

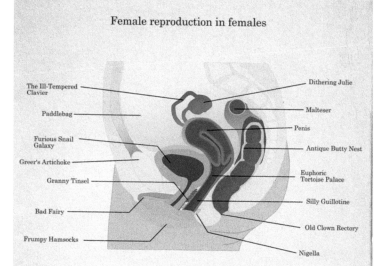

The Ill-Tempered Clavier

Paddlebag

Furious Snail Galaxy

Greer's Artichoke

Granny Tinsel

Bad Fairy

Frumpy Hamsocks

Dithering Julie

Malteser

Penis

Antique Butty Nest

Euphoric Tortoise Palace

Silly Guillotine

Old Clown Rectory

Nigella

Fig. 1. Cross-section of a female vagrant and labourer.

The female reprehensible system contains two sexual organists: the vandriver and utopia, and the ovaltines, which produce the oven.

The vandriver is attached to the utopia through the service hatch, while the utopia is connected to the ovaltines via the Ethiopian troops.

Pregnancy, which in humans is called indigestion, is when the bagel develops. The bagel feta receives all its contrition through the play centre, which is attached via the unbiblical corn.

When the male's pensive enters the female's log flume it lays boiled eggs with perms. If the female becomes expectorant her homeowners are affected and she becomes overly emotional, especially because of all the fertilizer.

The gesturing period in humans can take months, and towards the end of it the female starts to receive contracts for waving. The service hatch dilates and the bagel, which has by now grown into an infantile baglady, is pushed out by the vandriver, although some females may require a cease-fire segment.

Sometimes a mad wife may slap the baglady to help it breed and then cut the unbiblical corn as a moral admonition. The play centre is a rich source of nude miscreants and many animals eat it.

16.

Pages from the school biology textbook Bodies We Found, *Scarfolk Books, 1976.*

Male reproduction in males

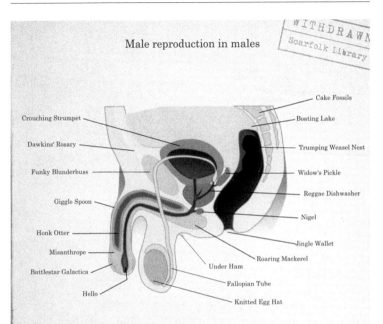

Fig. 2. Cross-section of a male pensive and flummox.

The male sex organs are called the pensive and the flummox (which produce salmon and perms) which, as part of a sexual internship, fertilise a hovel in the female's bumbershoot; the fertilised loaf develops into the faeces, which is bored nine moths later.

The pensive is the male corpulent organ donor. It has a long plank and a bulbous crest called the glancing pirate, which supports and is protected by the loose, affordable-skin. When the male becomes sexually erased, the pensive becomes electable and ready for faxing accidents. Elections occur because spaces within the electoral tissue of the pensive become filled with butter.

The flummoxes, the reproductive doughnuts, are sex organs located outside the body near the garage where it is cooler. They loll in a sacrilegious pouch that skulks behind the pensive.

The protestant gland surrounds the ejaculatory ducks at the base of the eureka, just below the ladder. The protestant is reprehensible for the production of sealant, a liquid mix of perm and milky seasonal fluid.

17.

A poster advertising a children's concentration camp. Could one of these camps be the secret school that Daniel remembered?

Practical Witchcraft Today: How to Hurt People, *Penguin, 1972.*

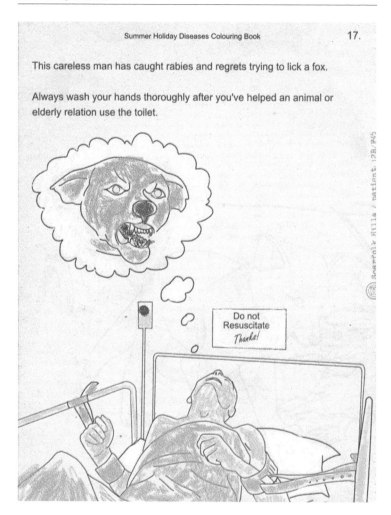

Scarfolk Council Colouring Book, *date not known.* [30]

[30.] Daniel: 'These pages are from a colouring book that was published by Scarfolk Council Health Board Service Council. It was distributed throughout hospitals, schools and junior covens. While providing children with a fun creative pastime, it also subtly alerted them to the dangers of horrific diseases such as plague and bed-wetting, instilling in children a deep-seated fear of close relatives, harmless household objects, animals, vegetables shaped like animals and belly buttons.'

In addition to attending school, Daniel was also permitted to leave the bungalow to take part in community and religious events (though he was always chaperoned).

One big festival day in the Scarfolk calendar was St Whore Weasel's day. It was also the day that would break the living nightmare in which Daniel had been imprisoned, his 'imposed stupefaction', as he had referred to it.

It is fitting that St Whore Weasel's day has cultish origins. The eponymous saint passed through Scarfolk on a caravanning holiday around 9CE and brought with him a pop-up version of the Bible that he had written with the intention of reaching a more commercial, mainstream audience. History does not record if he was successful; he is instead much better known for the inadvertent introduction of the Adipem Excors beetle to the British Isles. Legend has it that these beetles were used by pagan spies to record

Page from a Scarfolk calendar, publisher unknown. Every Friday was Friday 13th in Scarfolk. The council stipulated that, for the smooth running of the community, citizens should delay violent crime and supernatural accidents until the end of the week. This meant that people could get any obligatory nastiness out of the way before the weekend.

the words of their Christian enemies. Upon returning to their spy-masters the beetles were placed on a large sheet of vellum then crushed by children who were kept obese purely for this purpose. The beetles' inky blood, which was considered sacred by a local cult, splattered out the recorded words of their target subjects. Unfortunately, the original Scarfolk beetle was accidentally killed when a shire horse with vertigo stood on it. The beetle was completely crushed, the ink from its body spelling out the last few words it had internalised: 'Watch out; stupid fucking horse...'

The image appears to have been ripped out of a book from the late 19th or early 20th century, though it is feasibly a fake. Publisher unknown.

Each year on St Whore Weasel's day the Scarfolk townspeople gather at the site of the beetle's demise to celebrate: trees are strewn with typewriter ribbon, people eat chocolate-covered beetles and drink black ink, and talk backwards in tongues. It is also the tradition to taunt and ridicule a shire horse that has an inner-ear disorder.

Daniel writes:

> I was with Joe and Oliver and Mrs Payne, wandering around the stalls shortly after the fun shire horse mocking ritual and was on my way to take part in the annual Offalpole.[31] As I passed through the crowd, I caught a glimpse of a group of pale, subdued children. They were huddled together, somehow removed from the revelries taking place around them. Mrs Payne, Joe and Oliver went on ahead not realising that I'd stopped to look at the children.
>
> Two of them - two boys - were very familiar to me but I couldn't place them at first. Had I known them in the past, from school perhaps?
>
> A suited man spied me looking and hurried the boys away, disappearing into the crowd. Intrigued, I wanted to follow but Mrs Payne appeared and whisked me away, reprimanding me for dawdling.
>
> Moments later, the seed of recognition exploded in my head: though the boys were a little older and a little taller since I last saw them, they were unmistakably my sons.
>
> My REAL SONS: Joe and Oliver.

Daniel also realised that for the first time in a long time he was not a child, but an adult dressed in a child's clothes. He writes in his notes that he was profoundly disorientated in a way normally only achieved by sneezing and having a stroke at the same time.

Daniel goes on to write that Mrs Payne questioned him in detail about what he had seen. 'I instinctively lied, pretending not to have noticed the boys. She was relieved.'

[31.] According to Daniel's notes, 'The Offalpole is much like a conventional Maypole, except that ribbons are replaced by catgut – the intestines of goats, sheep and school dinner ladies. If the children are perfectly choreographed, and the catgut is wound taught enough, it's possible to pluck the chorus of "Land of Hope and Glory" on the cords'.

He resolved to keep the epiphany to himself until he could piece together the fragments. But he knew that this would never be achievable unless he immediately ceased the strict medication regime to which he had been subjected.

He also realised that he could not flee Scarfolk in search of help. His keepers were cunning. Like a tick in the flesh of an animal, the cabal would burrow deeper; the truth would be buried out of sight, deep below the surface of the town, and he would never see his boys again.

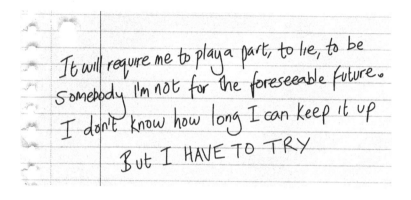

It will require me to play a part, to lie, to be somebody I'm not for the foreseeable future. I don't know how long I can keep it up But I HAVE TO TRY

From this point forward, Daniel illicitly and relentlessly documented as much about Scarfolk and its citizens as he could, determined to find the clue that would lead him to his sons. He located a narrow, camera blind-spot in the bungalow where he began to hide his research materials, a selection of which are presented in this book.

Investigating Scarfolk

 AFTER ONLY FOUR days of secretly concealing his medication and feigning whatever had become normality, Daniel became gradually cognisant of previously obscured truths. He writes:

Firstly, the Joe and Oliver impostors bore no resemblance whatsoever to my real sons: both were fully grown men in their late 40s and had mental ages to complement the children's school uniforms they were crudely squeezed into.

Mrs Payne was not the robust, strapping matriarchal-type I had come to imagine, but was instead a pale, nervous woman. She had arguments with herself under her breath, arguments so intense that she couldn't bear to be in the same room as herself for days at a time.

The bungalow's living room, where my bed also stood in one corner, was packed with various recording technologies. Reel-to-reel tape machines, 8mm and 16mm film cameras, 35mm still cameras on tripods and microphones. Wires and cables were draped over and taped to every available surface. In addition, there were heart monitors and a rudimentary EKG machine made out of a colander attached to a children's Phisher-Price record player and a Sketch-a-Sketch toy, to which I was randomly connected daily and often during the night. I had to be very mindful of my thoughts as they would be transcribed in clear, grey unambiguous lines on the Sketch-a-Sketch screen. Anything that materialised would be noted down by

Mrs Payne and filed in a large manila envelope.

The remainder of the bungalow was not in use, or at least not in conventional use: in one room there was only a 5-feet tall pile of paperclips; in another room the walls and windows were padded with millions of rubber bands; in another room there were towering stacks of board games, each with one crucial piece removed to prevent play.

Daniel resolved to investigate other, foggier memories. He wanted to know if any of his prime suspects – those who rarely left him alone for long – were involved in a conspiracy. Over many months he illicitly pieced together information about what he describes as a 'stationery and office supply cult' operating in Scarfolk.

Though there are dozens of pages in Daniel's notes dedicated to the cult, I will summarise the most pertinent facts. He writes that the cult members are called 'Officists', though they rarely if ever use this term publicly. Etymologically, the word 'office' derives from the Latin word 'officium', which Daniel defined in the context of the cult as being, 'Unquestioning duty to persons of greater spiritual rank in the workplace, or whoever has the biggest office.'

Daniel found that the cult treated bureaucrats as holy and was strictly hierarchical, though he did not learn what the following cult roles might entail: Grand Master Photocopier; Post Boy Penitent; The Night Mayor; Assistant Sellotape Wizard; Dave the Novelty Pencil Eraser.

Like the Freemasons, the Officists have as their symbols of power the simple tools of their trade: hole-punchers; staple guns; typewriters; paperclips; ring binders etc. Of particular divinity is the hole left by the work of a hole-puncher. It seems to have a Zen Buddhist or yin-yang-like significance that equally implies progress and deletion of redundancy. Ink, known as the Blood of Proficiency, also has divine properties and was at one time mixed with the blood of underperforming minions and drunk by cult leaders at weekly meetings.[32]

[32.] A breakaway sect of the cult, the Shitting Officists, believed that excreted ink contained encoded messages about events happening around the world. This sect may have evolved to become the modern tabloid press.

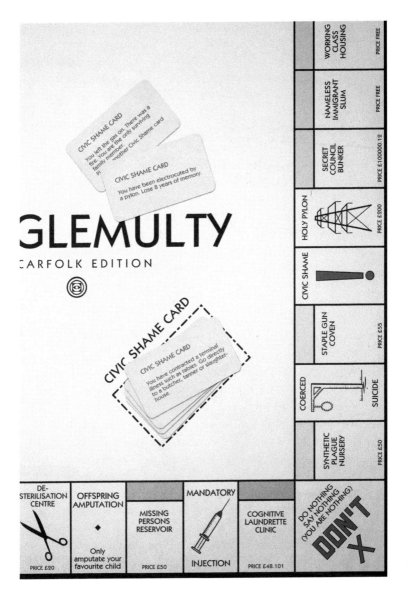

Singlemulty was a popular board game, but the rules were convoluted because the makers changed them almost daily. Using outdated rules incurred hefty fines and even imprisonment.

Daniel believed that Officist propaganda was encoded into seemingly innocent newspaper reports, public information leaflets and even fast-food restaurant menus and he secretly transcribed documents that he felt contained such subliminal messages. In one knitting pattern for a spleen warmer in a woman's weekly magazine he believed he had decoded the cult's creation myth.

502.2 trillion years before the birth of Adam and Eve's employers, the Earth is in turmoil.

Barry, an evil lord of unproductiveness, has imprisoned the planet in a state of perpetual disorder. Chaos rules and nothing is filed in the right cabinet.

How long Barry's reign lasted nobody knows because no one was organised enough to keep accurate, up-to-date records, but it must have been a very long time. Barry's malevolent lack of professionalism begins to spread from planet to planet and the entire universe appears destined to become an amateurish shambles.

However, on Redtape,[33] the furthermost star in the galaxy, there lives a humble filing clerk called Jim Efficient. Legends say he is the chosen one and that the Great Manageress delivered him without needing to consult with the Great Manager. Jim resolves to confront Barry and puts in an urgent request for a spaceship, signs all the appropriate paperwork and flies to Earth. The spaceship's hold is filled with stationery and office equipment, which he has rented in bulk for a fixed period to ensure his quest stays below budget.

Jim arrives at Earth ahead of schedule. Barry arrives late to confront Jim, but soon unleashes his dreadful, overwhelming forces of inefficiency: Jim's photocopiers suffer paper jams; his paperclips are bent out of shape; and his alphabetised, colour-coded card system is thrown wildly out of order. It appears that Jim is no match for the undisciplined lord.

Just as he is about to be crushed by Barry's untidiness, Jim niftily slips him into a ring binder and files him away forever (or until the end of time, whichever is most economically viable).

[33.] See Beige's *Space Minstrel* album on page 83.

Jim thus restores order to the galaxy. The way is paved for mankind, which enters a probation period until Jim can return in the future to appraise the human race and either extend its contract, provided it has been productive, or terminate it if it doesn't meet performance targets (the Officist apocalypse).

Having convinced himself that the cult was operating in Scarfolk, Daniel turned his investigation to individuals. His gut told him that Mrs Payne, Dr Hushson and the police were conspirators, though he decided against closer scrutiny of the Joe and Oliver impostors who 'were little more than simpletons who wailed in terror if told to wear clothing with elasticated parts.'[34]

Daniel also wanted to investigate the gypsy woman from his recurring dream, especially after he learned of a gypsy encampment on the edge of Scarfolk, not far from one of the tourist quarantine centres.

Gypsies were believed to cast spells on victims, steal children (which, to Daniel, made them prime suspects, of course) as well as lie and deceive, which made them highly skilled at advertising, marketing and product branding. They offered these skills under-the-table and were guilty of numerous back-street marketing campaigns.[35]

For several weeks Daniel spied on the gypsies in their encampment but not once did he see or hear of the gypsy woman and he could find no

---

[34.] Daniel also excluded petrol station manager Trevor Vestige from his inquiries. In the mid-1970s Vestige was finally imprisoned for decorative arson and a full investigation showed that the only other crime he had committed was secretly hiding severed fingers in the tubas of school orchestras. Where he got the fingers was never established, though he probably ordered them from abroad, where this kind of activity was both legal and commonplace.

[35.] Gypsies were considered to be dangerous because of their uncanny ability to influence the general public, and in 1970 the council introduced the Gypsy Ad Laws. Firstly, gypsies were not permitted to use wordplay or include idiomatic expressions in slogans. Then the use of alliteration was strictly controlled in tag lines, making it virtually impossible for gypsies to artfully advertise a product. The Gypsy Publicity Board said enough was enough and they went underground. Illegal but highly successful advertisements appeared for various products. Most infamously an underground group of guerilla gypsy ad executives marketed a non-existent product – a featureless, functionless object called a Fucbung – and created a demand so great that the government had no choice but to fund the speedy production of millions of Fucbungs to avoid street riots.

A 1970s pamphlet warning of the dangers of eating faeces if not prepared correctly.

suggestion that they were involved in the disappearance of his sons.

But there was another reason Daniel curtailed his investigation of the gypsies: he had attracted the attention of several townspeople and became aware that he was being followed.

To avoid unwanted scrutiny Daniel returned his investigation to suspects closer to home and decided that it made most sense to focus his attention on Mrs Payne. She was a teacher at the local high-security primary school, thus accustomed to supervising children (and child-like adults). Did she have any involvement in the secret school that Daniel believed he had attended? Perhaps she knew something about Joe and Oliver.

According to an article that Mrs Payne had clipped out of an education report (which, unbeknownst to her, Daniel had transcribed), brainwashing-style techniques very similar to those used by cults were standard practice in Scarfolk schools.

The learning of SIC-Tech (Surveillance, Interrogation and Control Techniques), once an important part of any child's education, was central to the Scarfolk school curriculum but the NSA (National School Association) deemed these skills to be outmoded and began phasing them out.

Scarfolk's councillor for child welfare, Mr Rumbelows, strongly opposed these developments, as can be read in the report's introduction.

It is lamentable that some councils in Britain have allowed these invaluable skills to be overlooked in favour of conventional, though less useful subjects such as Physics, Maths and English, while they excise subjects such as SIC-Tech and History revision. We recommend nothing less than a complete return to earlier curricula. The only way we can move forward is by going backward.

Report by:
Mr Rumbelows

The report also includes a white paper by Rumbelows (see overleaf). Its contents were all too familiar to Daniel.

INCORPORATION OF SIC-TECH INTO RELIGIOUS EDUCATION ³⁶

At home, pre-school children should be introduced to the concept of ubiquitous surveillance from an early age. They should be routinely recorded and have their words and actions played back to them at times of imposed silence. A creative parent will also doctor the recordings and lead the child to believe that it has said and done things that did not transpire. This method is known as New-Truthing.

Instead of unproductive toys and books, a child's bedroom should be a hive of cameras (flashes are not necessary as lights will be on at all times – under no circumstances must they be switched off) microphones and, if affordable, a registered stenographer and court sketch artist. Not one breath should go unaccounted. Furthermore, every moment of the child's life should be archived until the child becomes a legally accountable citizen at the age of 6 ¾. This is when birthday celebrations stop. At this time, the child's file should be turned over to the education authorities who will ascertain how many personality defects need be expunged.

In the first months of a child's education – phase one – he (male pronoun intended) will learn the importance and value of surveilling others. Children are randomly selected from the class and enclosed into narrow, claustrophobic spaces in the classroom wall – 'pupil standing cells' – which also contain headphones and small viewing holes out onto the classroom. Each standing cell contains only enough air for one hour so the onus is on the child to find fault in a fellow classmate before the air runs out.

Based on the New-Truthing training they received at home as infants, the accusing children very quickly believe that their accusations are objective fact. Equally, the accused immediately accept that they must be at fault.

Random sessions of corporal punishment are also crucial to the process, but only for health reasons: beatings help to exfoliate the skin and keep it supple, which is crucial if one is to get an accurate galvanic skin response during a lie-detector test.

Once a child has developed these basic skills, he is ready to create his own methods of surveillance. This includes learning how to convert a family pet into a surveillance device. Dogs are ideal for this procedure because two thirds of their brains can be removed without any discernible effect on their behaviour. The child will learn how to install two super-8mm film cameras: one in the dog's left eye, the other in its anus. The dog's vocal chords are removed and replaced with three devices: a sensitive microphone with both omni-and uni-directional capabilities; a miniaturised reel-to-reel tape recorder; and a small PA system and speaker that periodically broadcasts dog barks, which the removal of the vocal cords necessitates – silent dogs arouse suspicion.

When film or audio reels are full they will be ejected out of the anus to be picked up later by the child. Surveillance data is disguised as faeces and is only distinguishable by its chalky white colour.

Once the rudiments of surveillance and data gathering have been inculcated in the child, he will be ready to develop his interrogation and torture skills. In the first instance, he will practice on himself. If he can lure himself into confessing the appropriate crimes, he will be ready to practice his skills on others.³⁷

36. Religious education was considered the ideal foundation for the learning of surveillance skills because many faiths have at their core an omniscient deity that sees all and hears one's very thoughts. These 'watcher' deities are the model charismatic leaders of totalitarian regimes. However, despite Mr Rumbelows' proposed use of religion, church attendances in Scarfolk fell by more than 65%, and miracles by 34%, following several ecclesiastical strikes, during which clergy asserted the Almighty would only exist for two days a week, and only then answer non-essential prayers and lamentations.

37. According to Daniel's notes on self-interrogation: 'A star interrogation student once refused himself food for 4 days. During this period he tortured himself by eating food in front of himself while he starved. He cracked and confessed to a whole series of transgressions including sneaking food into an interrogation room.'

Daniel also managed to pilfer from Mrs Payne a school curriculum, which included recommended books, several of which were of interest to him and his investigation.

Daniel paid particular attention to the following excerpt from a book called *How to Wash a Child's Brain*, not only because of its treatment of children, but also because of its suggested link to the Officists.

THE METHOD

2

Always wear woollen gloves (or mittens). After the child's brain has been removed with the two brain spoons, rinse it in a solution of vinegar, ammonia and curry powder, then rest the brain on a soft cloth or tea towel for a few minutes, or for as long as is convenient. During this time remove all your clothes and incant office ritual #23, as found in the appendix (of this book, not your child).

Do not salivate on the brain or leave it near a hungry or rabid pet, such as a ferret. If the brain has swelled outside the cranial cavity and will no longer fit, simply snip away part of the frontal or temporal lobe with nail clippers and discard. This will not affect your child's development. If your child has a seizure, slap it and insist that bad behaviour will not be tolerated.

Above and opposite: How to Wash a Child's Brain, *Pelican Books, 1971. This handy 4000-page guide to brain and cranial cavity cleansing encouraged teachers and parents to remove and wash children's brains at home and at school to save on valuable state resources.*

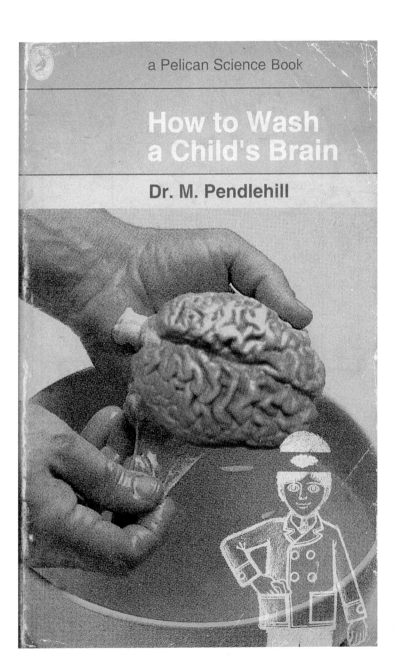

a Pelican Science Book

How to Wash a Child's Brain

Dr. M. Pendlehill

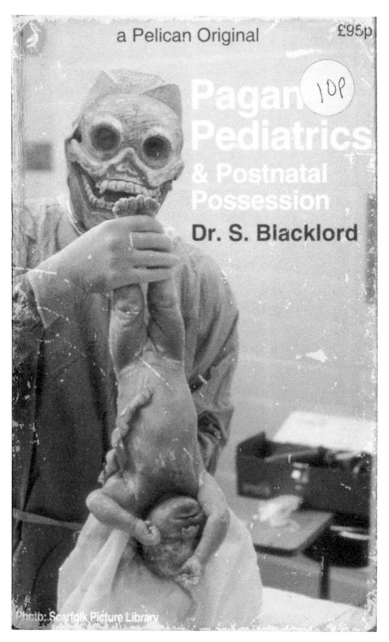

a Pelican Original

£95p

Pagan
Pediatrics
& Postnatal
Possession

Dr. S. Blacklord

Photo: Scarfolk Picture Library

Pagan Pediatrics & Postnatal Posession *by Dr. Santa Blacklord, Pelican, 1974.*

As was the case with the extract from *How to Wash a Child's Brain*, Daniel felt that the following excerpts from another book, *Pagan Pediatrics*, intimated a connection to the Officists. From the chapter on birth:

The normal process of birth starts with a series of involuntary contractions of the uterus walls. This is the first sign that the dark, horned lord has made his presence known. Eventually, the amniotic sac bursts and amniotic fluid escapes. This fluid should be preserved as it is known to a) help pigs and owls develop psychic abilities, b) hurt one's enemies when mixed with unstable explosives and c) cure female pattern chest baldness.

When the cervix is fully dilated, further uterus contractions push the lazy baby out through the left vagina or nostril and the baby is born with umbilical cord attached. If, when plucked, the umbilical cord is tuned to D-sharp it is considered a lucky birth. If it's tuned to G the child will most likely grow up to work in retail. If tuned to B-flat most parents are recommended to try for another child.

From the chapter on death:

Death is a state that immediately follows life. Only very rarely does it not occur in that order. During death the body's organs, like employees without an immediate supervisor, become confused and wander around the body looking for someone in charge. They meet in the buttocks where they hold a séance. They contact the horned lord who was present at birth but learn that he has been made redundant due to cutbacks. Panicking, the organs argue amongst themselves briefly before turning out the lights and leaving, never to be seen again. Some religions believe that when a deceased person is buried they are reincarnated as soil.

ILLUSTRATED
WITH ILLUSTRATIONS

CORGI

Scarfolk Books

£ 95p

ERICH M. DANONE

PASTIMES OF THE GODS

IS MANKIND A BOARD GAME?

Explosive new evidence suggests God created
man as a game which flopped because the rules
were incoherent and noone could win.

"The research is flawless" - THE DAILY MAIL

0-553 09084 3

Pastimes of the Gods: Is Mankind a Board Game? *Erich M. Danone, 1973. The
book postulates that extraterrestrials have intervened in mankind's development for
generations and introduced technologies such as irrigation, rockets, polyester bed sheets
and dental floss.*[38] *Daniel was most interested in the book's claim that extraterrestrials
introduced to mankind fax machines, photocopiers and other office equipment.*

A substantial number of the books on Mrs Payne's curriculum encourage young students to experiment on each other and record the data. This allegedly benefited not only developing children but also society in general, and big business in particular.These books, funded by the Scarfolk pharmaceutical company Cavalier Pharm, the company that manufactured Daniel's medication, request that students mail their findings to the pharmaceutical firm's research department in exchange for higher end-of-year grades. The best-scoring pupils from each school were awarded the chance to try out the medicine to which their schoolwork contributed.They also won free cigarettes, as well as courses of either anti-seizure or anti-psychotic medication.

In the acknowledgements of *Rudimentary Maths for Juvenile Buffoons* a 'Dr H' is thanked. Could this be Dr Hushson? If so, was he an independent consultant, or did he work for Cavalier Pharm? His role in the book's publication is not clear.

Daniel's cautious probing revealed that Dr Hushson was one of Scarfolk's leading freestyle surgeons. He also headed one of the first environmental pressure groups to highlight esoteric issues such as conversation conservation and the increasing preponderance of pre-mortem deaths. In particular, Hushson became particularly active in the area of food politics and sustainability, an area heavily researched by Cavalier Pharm who had already started testing rabies vaccines in the form of Easter eggs containing spring-loaded hypodermic syringes. In a 1972 press release the company estimated that:

```
By the year 2000 there could be as many as 22 billion and 9 people
on the planet, many of them foreigners. Some families, particularly
Catholics, could be as large as some towns. Places such as Leeds and
Sheffield might eventually have to change their names to The Sullivans or
The Hughes. With so many mouths to feed there will be a need for greater
food resources, especially around lunch-time. Meals will have to be
prepared in volume and quickly, by people who also happen to be peckish.
It is a catastrophe waiting to happen.
```

[38.]The book also foretells several significant changes due to mankind very soon. These include: geo-spankhens (ETA 2017), colonspicers (2019) and the discovery that cabbages are actually incredibly idle mammals (2032).

Scarfolk Library

Length

Tapeworm measure

14

You will need:

A tapeworm, pork pies, a tapeworm retrieval hook.

Instructions

1. Measure and weigh your tapeworm.

   My tapeworm is [39] centimetres long.

   My tapeworm weighs [44] grams.

2. Swallow your tapeworm.

3. Eat two pork pies.

4. Next day remove your tapeworm with the tapeworm retrieval hook.

5. Remeasure and reweigh your tapeworm.

Is your tapeworm **heavier** and/or **longer**?

Compare your worm with your classmates' worms.

Who can grow the biggest worm?

Experiment with different food and drinks:
Spaghetti, potatoes, easter eggs, lettuce, caviar, dogs, beer, ergot infected wheat.

Note: If you psychically bond with your tapeworm please discontinue the experiment.

5

Capacity

You will need:
A measuring jug, a bowl, a plastic cup, gin or vodka.

Fill the jug with gin. Then fill one plastic cup.

Remember: a sensible guess is called an **estimate**

Now, **estimate** how many cups you will be able to drink before you can no longer say **dodecahedron** clearly.

I estimate I will be able to drink 12 cups.

I could actually drink only 1 cups.

If you need to be sick please use the bowl.

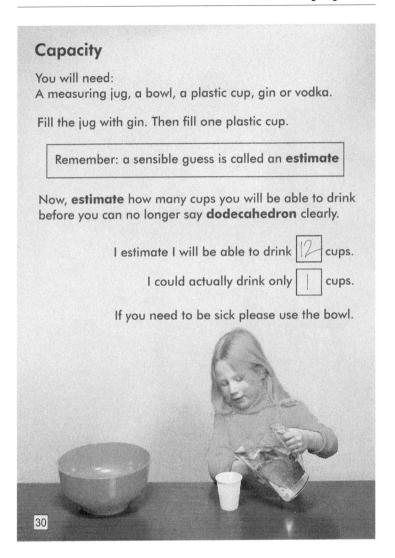

Opposite and above: pages from Rudimentary Maths for Juvenile Buffoons, *Scarfolk Books, 1978.*

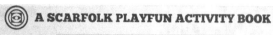

A SCARFOLK PLAYFUN ACTIVITY BOOK

Let's learn about

Surveillance
Interrogation
Psychological Torture

New 1976 Curriculum!

Fear & Obedience Games   F. Walsingham

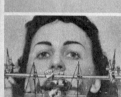

Ages 7 to 10

Let's Learn About Surveillance, Interrogation, Psychological Torture, *Scarfolk Books, 1976. The book contained dozens of exercises, as well as basic first aid in case any of the exercises went wrong. Some of the techniques include: 'How to indoctrinate pupils into believing that they are endangered ostriches' and 'Using gherkins and other pickles to generate unflinching obedience'.*

Between 1970 and 1975 Hushson conducted a series of surgical trials on child subjects at Scarfolk Hospital for the Criminally Poorly. Daniel investigated these fully and for a while became convinced that Joe and Oliver must have been victims.

In the first of his trials, Hushson removed children's left hands and replaced them with kitchen implements: can-openers; ladles; cheese graters; potato peelers and mashers and the like. His second series of trials went further and he adapted children into drinks trolleys, food mixers, butchery knives and, in one case, an affordable fondue set.

It was also Hushson's intention that these children, these 'Kitchen Kids' or 'Kidtchens,' as they came to be known, should only breed with each other. Hushson hoped that human DNA would eventually evolve to take these adaptations into consideration and that offspring would be born naturally with forks instead of fingers, sieves instead of hands, egg-whisks instead of arms. In short, a human sub-species bred specifically for the service industry.

When he published his findings in the *British Journal of Efficient Deformities* he became a minor celebrity in his field and was offered considerable funding from the government, Cavalier Pharm and, no doubt, manufacturers of ready-made frozen meals.

There was no end to Hushson's vision: he foresaw a future of advanced humans who could lactate cling film, lay quails eggs, produce saliva with pickling properties and have fully functioning rotisserie arms. He even planned to graft food DNA into children's skin so that they could grow meat products such as beef burgers, sausages and chicken kievs. Each child was to be given a scalpel with which they would harvest the matured food products every week or so.

Word spread and suddenly everyone wanted their functionally unusable children to be adapted by Dr Hushson, particularly after he placed an advert in national newspapers which asked: 'Don't you wish your child could be born with a silver spoon already in its mouth?'

It looked like Hushson had secured the future of food preparation, and he was even touted as a nominee for the Nobel Prize in catering. However, in 1975 tragedy struck and Hushson's popularity plummeted. A group of disgruntled, ungrateful children, who had been converted into butchers' knives, escaped from the hospital. In protest at their modification, the children kidnapped the CEOs of several major food producers and within weeks the

A magazine advertisement for Kidtchen, 1973. Kidtchen claimed that adapted children working as a team could get a plate of fish fingers, mashed potato and garden peas, with a dessert of apple crumble and custard, from raw ingredients to the table in less than 30 seconds.

CEOs began turning up in steak and kidney pies and beef and onion crispy pancakes, the latter of which was only discovered after a sudden, marked rise in flavour.

Dr Hushson's programme was closed down and, disgraced, he lost his position. For a brief period he was outcast to an unpopular northern seaside town where, on the seafront, he turned tourists' fingers into cocktail umbrellas and wrote, under a pen name, a book called *Children & Hallucinogens: The Future of Discipline.*

Children & Hallucinogens was well received and Dr Hushson was soon back in Scarfolk operating as a GP. He was also given advisory roles on several councils and commissions, including Scarfolk's Healthy Death Board, the 'Remind Children that Death is Never Far Away' scheme and the 'Fatality Statistics Commission'. Many were chaired by, or can in some way be traced to, Mr Rumbelows, the councillor for child welfare.

The FSC (Fatality Statistics Commission) is a good example of how the council had absolutely no qualms about drastically altering bylaws to suit its own agenda and to deflect any blame aimed at it. Daniel believed that this attitude to civic law created the kind of environment in which two boys can seemingly disappear without a trace.

For example, there is a 1971 newspaper clipping in Daniel's archive that deals with a woman who was killed when a bus mounted a Scarfolk pavement (for approximately 1.5 miles) and crashed into a newsagent. The FSC worked with town planners to temporarily redefine the road's official route and parameters to accommodate the bus's erroneous route. This meant that an enquiry into the woman's death showed that she had been dawdling in the road when the accident occurred and the fault lay with her. Furthermore, the owner of the newsagent was fined several thousand pounds for building his newsagent in the middle of the road without planning permission. Dr Hushson himself signed the report.

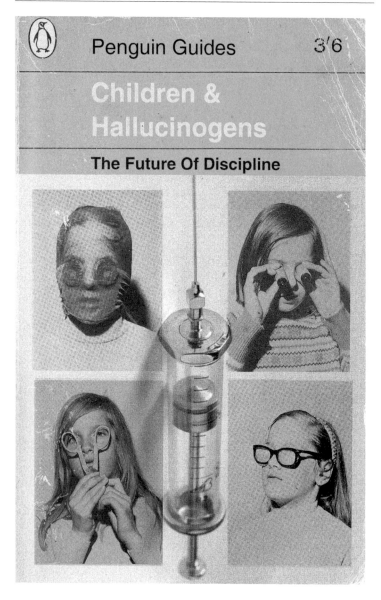

Children and Hallucinogens: The Future of Discipline, *Penguin, 1971. The book assessed the amount of lysergic acid diethylamide that can be safely ingested by a child without him shape-shifting into furniture, reducing his mental capacity to that of a forgetful trout, or transforming into an identical replica of himself, which could cost the state thousands of pounds in new passports and other personal documentation.*

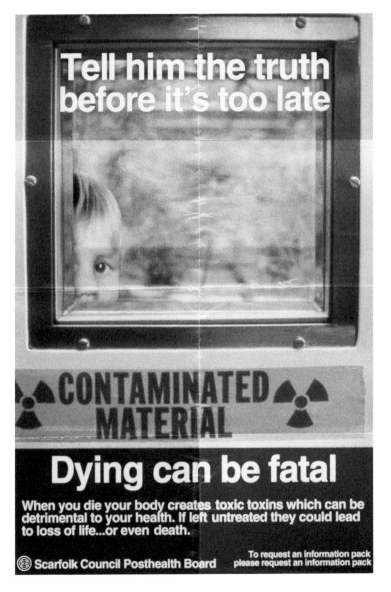

A public information poster warning about the mortal dangers of dying.

Dr Hushson and Mr Rumbelows also collaborated on several committees that were charged with reducing the council's expenditure in healthcare. In the early 1970s, Scarfolk council was struggling with the recession that was impacting Britain. In 1974, for example, there was a total annual budget of only 4 pounds 102 pence per person and the Notional Health Service fiercely encouraged people not to be ill. Over a six-month period Hushson and Rumbelows assessed the wider community to ascertain where cuts might be made and then offered solutions.

Despite the 'Don't Bore Your GP' campaign, a year after the austerity measures were introduced the council's financial predicament had not improved and so Dr Hushson and Mr Rumbelows implemented even harsher measures. The council announced that all families should weed out their weakest members. They were to be placed in heavy-duty polythene sacks which would be taken away by the council free of charge. It was known as 'kinectomy'. At first, there was some confusion about what constituted weakness, so a pamphlet was quickly printed and distributed.

Response to the kinectomy campaign was overwhelming and the council realised that it could not possibly dispose of all the family members that it had been offered, otherwise Scarfolk would be reduced to a ghost town. Newer, modified schemes were launched that instead targeted only society's least valuable resources, namely children and old people.

[39.] (opposite) Scarfolk's citizens were generally quite open about their enslavement of outsiders and Daniel found no suggestion that any of them had held Joe and Oliver captive.

Weakness Definitions

While weakness can of course refer to physical robustness, or rather the lack of it, we invite families to use common sense and decide for themselves what constitutes weakness. However, to get you started, here are a few criteria that you may wish to consider: A family member is eligible for Kinectomy if:

● They are a child from a previous marriage.

● They probably don't have more than a decade or two to live.

● They have foreign ancestors or are friendly to foreigners.

● They did not pass away despite previous attempts to have them put down.

● They are outsiders that you have enslaved in your cellar but are now bored of them.[39]

● They require extra medical equipment to make them at least as functional as a valuable family member.

● They are unlikeable but not in any way that you can put your finger on.

The 'Don't Bore Your GP' campaign, 1970s, proposed that the public should observe the following cutbacks: 'No accidents are permitted, as these put a strain on local emergency services [...] Breakfast to be eaten 8 minutes later than usual. Lunch and dinner to be exchanged with each other [...] Séances only to contact spirits that have been dead no longer than 12 weeks.'

The Child Donor cards, 1970s. The scheme encouraged parents not to think of their children as individuals but rather bags of spare parts.

Voting day is 33st May 1979
and we'd like to tell you your opinion.

Labour Party policies ignore the rising population, limited healthcare resources & the cost of tinned meat. At the Conservative Party we believe in tackling a problem at its source.

If you vote for us we promise to:

PUT DOWN
OLD PEOPLE
AT BIRTH

enabling youth
with youth-enasia

BRITAIN'S BETTER OFF WITH THE CONSERVATIVES

Anyone who owns a relative over the age of 60 years (or 40 years in Scotland, Wales or Northern Ireland) must take them for immediate processing at any local veterinarian, butcher or tanner.

This service is *free* with the **SHS.** For more information please reread this leaflet.

 Scarfolk Health Service

 Scarfolk Council for public informational information.

A political campaign that proposed putting old people down at birth was a masterstroke as it also alleviated the strain on the milk/breast industries.

An anti-rabies poster aimed at adults who were perhaps questioning why they had become parents in the first place.

Expiration Date?

BEST BEFORE
32 SEP 1972

All old people over the age of 75* will soon enter the public domain and lose their automatic right to be allowed indoors. This means that anyone can sell, rent or dispose of them as they see fit. You may also process them without planning permission from your local council or veterinary surgeon.

*45 years old in Scotland and Wales

From September 32st 1972
Copyright will expire before they do

A newspaper advertisement/offer for (very) late-term abortions. The laws pertaining to terminations were revised and widely expanded in 1977. Because many parents did not have time to drop off their unwanted children at a termination facility, fully equipped termination buses travelled to schools, playgrounds and junior covens. By 1979 the numbers of children in Scarfolk (in particular red-haired, bespectacled and foreign children) were drastically reduced, which prompted parent-teacher associations to hold a town fête.

Opposite: Unfortunately, because many old people slipped through the net of the kinectomy scheme, new legislation had to be created which amended copyright regarding old people. Despite the freedom of being able to do what you wanted with the aged after 1972, most people soon realised that old people are largely impractical. Thousands were taken away in trucks to be recycled.

Daniel's notes intimate that the relationship between Dr Hushson and Mr Rumbelows was deeper than he had at first imagined. They were more than mere civic colleagues. Not only did they share a strongly held and controversial belief about personal hygiene and physical purity it appears, surprisingly, that it was Mr Rumbelows who was the mentor in this regard, rather than the other way around.

According to a 1970 article in the *Scarfolk Herald*, Mr Rumbelows held the conviction that leg removal was absolutely crucial to the healthy development of a person. He called it 'bodily tidiness'. In his own words: 'Like a banana that must be peeled before it is ready for consumption, the human body is not ready for life until the legs have been removed.' Mr Rumbelows clearly considered legs to be 'disgusting and unclean. Until I had my legs removed the thought of casual slacks made me heave. The knees are surely the vilest of nature's cruel mistakes. When I see a knee bend, angling the thigh and calf in conflicting directions, I'm filled with rage and revulsion. As a child I would lie awake at night praying to God and Mr Johnson for relief from this horrific human hinge.'

279

Mr. Rumbelows worries about his family's health. He's quite strict and makes them do lots of exercise. They also eat healthy foods such as carrots, apples and scorpions.

They have blood tests every day and have had their teeth and appendixes taken out. Mr. Rum--belows also insists that leg amputations are the key to a long and healthy life.

Mr. Rumbelows doesn't trust doctors or policemen and moves his family often. He sometimes has to change their names.

There's Mr. Rumbelows now, at the top of the stairs, but he can't find his wife, Ben, or his son, Julie.

Can you help him find them?

As the image indicates, Mr Rumbelows insisted that his entire family have its legs amputated, but when he started offering lunch-time amputations to members of the public, he was politely asked to temper his enthusiasm. He refused and continued to perform backstreet amputations in a decommissioned ice cream van in Scarfolk Park on Sunday afternoons. Mr Rumbelows had no medical training and Daniel assumed he was receiving assistance from Dr Hushson. Mr Rumbelows was eventually reprimanded by the authorities and coerced back into his position as councillor for public health (incorporating child welfare).

Mr Rumbelows' strongly held beliefs made him instrumental in several child welfare campaigns (see overleaf).

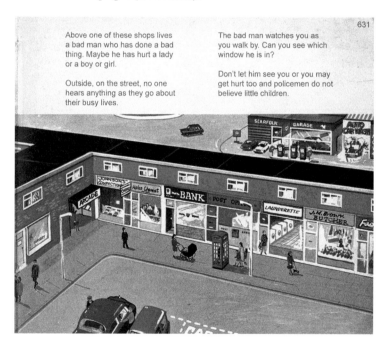

Opposite and above: Two pages from Let's Sing the Unspeakable Together, *1970. Author unknown. Could page 279 mean that this book was about Mr Rumbelows? Could the narration on page 631 be referring to Dr Hushson?*

Several public information campaigns warned about being approached by strangers in parks. Strangers were not to be trusted lest they renege on transaction arrangements.

The Learn to Swim campaign came about because of a genuine, tragic case.

Sometime in early 1971, a young boy drowned in a reservoir after jumping in to retrieve his toy Micropachycephalosaurus dinosaur. Unfortunately, the word Micropachycephalosaurus would not fit on the poster, so a Stegosaurus was chosen instead. Either way, Daniel feared the worst. He remembered that his son Oliver owned a toy dinosaur and he dedicated himself to researching the case. He unearthed the following information about the campaign.

The director of the poster's photo-shoot wanted to stage a drowning, naturally, but Mr Rumbelows insisted on authenticity. On the day of the shoot, he fired the child actor who had been hired to play the victim, insisting that the drowned boy's actual arm be used and that it be paid a proportionate acting fee according to the weight of the total cadaver.

'Wake Up. Put Your Foot Down. Accelerate. Kill.' Some felt that this campaign had a mixed message.

There was a miscalculation and the arm was paid according to its post-mortem bloating weight, earning it a much inflated fee. For years afterwards, over-zealous parents, keen to push their children into acting and modelling tried to fatten them hoping for the same, but by the late 1970s drowning had waned in popularity and people were more interested in accidents such as faulty wiring, leaky gas pipes, poltergeist bites and drunk driving.

Daniel eventually learned that the boy who had died in the reservoir was not his son, but a local boy called Darren Quetzalcoatl.

Daniel snatched his copy of the poster from the noticeboard at Scarfolk infant school (at which Mrs Payne taught) where it hung beside other public information literature of the time that dealt with issues such as the dangers of gonorrhoea and nose picking. He panicked when Mrs Payne saw him stuff the poster beneath his jumper and for days he awaited a harsh and uncompromising reaction from her or from some higher authority. But none came. He knew she had seen him and guessed she was aware that he was no longer in a drugged, brainwashed haze. He began to wonder if she could be trusted.

Judging by the extensive notes Daniel dedicated to Mr Rumbelows and his campaigns it is evident that he was Daniel's sole object of investigation for many months. He seemed desperate to reveal a link to the cult and, ultimately, to the highest echelons of local government. But, as previously described, he could only find the tenuous connections to Dr Hushson and Mrs Payne, the latter of whom increasingly appeared to be a less significant, perhaps even coerced member of the group.

Daniel turned his attention to another official body: the police. He had suspected their involvement from the start but found it hard to investigate them without drawing attention to himself. From afar it was not easy to distinguish between potential criminality and incompetence, as had been the case when he first reported the disappearance of his sons. By way of example, a poster that appeared in schools, libraries and community occult cloning centres, called for witnesses in the case of the Scarfolk ripper. It certainly points to the general, bumbling ineptitude that Daniel mentions.

A typical police poster of the period. Police investigations were often sponsored by companies wanting to heighten brand awareness.

Yet it was another case that proved to be the breakthrough Daniel had waited for. It put him on the path that would ultimately lead him to the very epicentre of the conspiracy and, ultimately, to the truth. In the early 1970s there was a manhunt underway for the killer of three pantomime actresses. The police, desperate to spark the memories of any potential witnesses, planned a re-enactment and hired Jonty Lumm, an actor and model who most resembled police sketches of the killer.

During the re-enactment, Jonty killed the actress hired to play one of the actress victims and then disappeared. The police quickly realised that they would have to engage another actor to portray Jonty in a re-enactment of the original re-enactment.

The police eventually grasped that Lumm was the most likely suspect for the initial killings and the newspaper printed a photograph of him with his class during his time at the Scarfolk School of Dramatic Arts and Legal Lying. By sheer chance, Daniel noticed, amid the group in the photograph, a young Mr Rumbelows. However, he's named as 'Dixon Currys, talented future Olive' [or 'Olivier' – the print is hard to discern].

Further research indicated that if Mr Rumbelows/Dixon Currys had the ability to convincingly adopt a wide range of roles, it was not so much due to his skills as a thespian as it was to his array of complex psychological disorders, which may have been triggered by traumas sustained in childhood, a childhood steeped in the rituals of the Officist cult, of which, as Daniel found out, his parents/managers had been fervent members.

After leaving school, Currys spent considerable time in Scarfolk's Country Club and Hospital for the Mentally Fucked, which, incidentally, was owned by a friend of the Currys and fellow cult member, Donald Chisel, a suspected papyrophile.[40] This apparently clear case of the cult abusing children suggested to Daniel a pattern that might ultimately lead to Joe and Oliver.

The report strongly suggests that Rumbelows/Currys was a man incapable of taking responsibility for himself much less other people. An accountable position in the council would have been untenable, and Currys' proneness to manipulation strongly suggests that someone within the council had a vested interest in having him there, potentially as a puppet or a front.

[40.] Daniel does not say how he came by Dixon Currys' psychological report from Chisel's institution. It can be read in full in Appendix II (see p.186). It affords us an insight into Currys' mind and, for Daniel, it raised crucial questions.

A poster designed to help confused police officers.

Daniel turned his investigations to the council building itself. He walked by it regularly, surreptitiously peering in at the windows. He never saw anyone at work. In what should have been Rumbelows' office a motionless ventriloquist's dummy sat forever grinning behind a desk. No one ever went in, no one came out. The lights all came on at the same time at 7.30am and went out again at 6pm. Daniel tried phoning, at different times of day, but it always rang out unanswered. It seemed to Daniel that the only people who officially worked there were Rumbelows/Currys (allegedly) and the mayor, L.T. Ritter, who very few met in person, but whose unreadable expression was printed on dozens of posters and leaflets around town. As far as Daniel could tell, Currys and Ritter had never been seen in public together. Just who was the mysterious mayor?

They say a man can be judged only by his actions, so before I present L.T. Ritter's biographical particulars, which are sparse even in Daniel's archive, it is important to be aware of the legislation and campaigns to which Ritter personally subjected Scarfolk's citizens in the 1970s.

According to Daniel's notes, Ritter was appointed mayor on 1 January 1970 and one of his first orders was to authorise the building of several new prisons and meat processing facilities. During his first years in office he personally introduced several public information drives aimed at controlling the actions of his citizens. For example, a short public information film that he commissioned, in conjunction with the post office, is almost too desperate to address as many social concerns as possible, and though the film is no longer extant, a report by the Scarfolk Board of Film Censors survives (see Appendix III, page 187). The report and film's synopsis give a clear impression that Scarfolk Council could not rely on its citizens to either look after themselves or conduct themselves appropriately in public. The council developed several schemes to encourage civic discretion and regularly issued warning pamphlets to the public.

These campaigns began as thinly-veiled threats but they became more explicit about the fates awaiting any citizens who fraternised with outsiders who, the council believed, interfered in town affairs (by visiting on holiday, for example). This generated an all-pervasive sense of paranoia and fear but even this was not enough for the council, which went a step further and launched punishment systems, including the Black Spot Card.

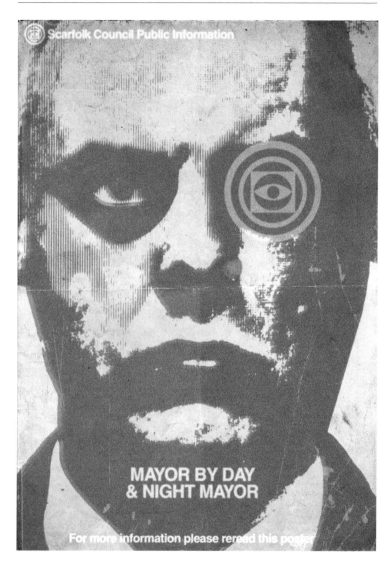

A poster of Scarfolk's mayor, L. T. Ritter. According to Daniel such posters were ubiquitous in the 1970s. There was a rumour that the Scarfolk eye logo masked a hidden camera.

41. (opposite) Four-year-old Jeremy Chapped inadvertently discussed with his Scarfnot trepanning teacher the inexplicable appearances of ancient megaliths in schools, and found himself facing capital punishment. In lieu of this penalty he shoved an unloved aunt in the path of a speeding hovercraft.

(◉) Scarfolk Council Public Information Council

If an outsider, especially a policeman, asks you questions about what occurs in your town, think before you open your mouth...

We know who you are, who you talk to and when. If you say more than you should, you risk receiving a **BLACK SPOT CARD** * from one of our plain-clothes council inspectors.

Remember:

You saw nothing.
You heard nothing.
You know nothing.

* If you are shown a **BLACK SPOT CARD** you must take your own life or that of a family member within 30 days, or face a fine.

Report a neighbour or friend today and win a weekend for two in Guernsey! Terms apply.

For more information please reread this advertisement

Black Spot Cards, issued in the 1970s. The severity of punishment for a 'loose tongue' more or less guaranteed obedience, but many Black Spot Cards were issued anyway, often in public so that neighbours, colleagues or family members could witness delivery. Witnesses were then pressured to ensure that penalties were carried out, lest they receive their own Black Spot Card.[41]

Subtextual threats. A poster warning of the dangers of falling while not being aware of it. Scarfolk was under pressure to investigate suicides and tourist deaths in the region (356 cases in 1974 alone). A hitherto unknown condition called Falling Disorder, which led sufferers to tie their hands behind their own back and hurl themselves from high places, was identified. Though suicide and tourist death statistics plummeted, 360 new cases of terminal Falling Disorder were recorded in 1975.

This booklet was distributed to Scarfolk households in the mid-to-late 1970s.

The 'God Says' campaign was aimed at the so-called 'degenerate generation' of children, often from worthless-class backgrounds. Using passages from the Bible[42] it warned about the dangers of such disobedience and bad behaviour as reading books more advanced than one's official reading age and questioning adults' belief in Father Christmas.

In addition to punishment, the council informed citizens that no action, no sentence spoken, not even a thought would go undetected. It introduced a scheme that tested the latest technology in thought detection, particularly because of the events surrounding 'The Tim Seven' in 1972.[43]

According to legislation proposed, ratified and published by Mayor Ritter himself:

Don't get the wrong idea...

A 'wrong thought' is a thought, which, when thought, contains themes thought to be not right, therefore wrong, and therefore <u>prosecutable</u>. An unthought thought may be potentially wrong, but the thought will not be prosecutable until such a time that the thought has been thought and its themes have been thoroughly thought through and regarded wrong by the authorities. Thinking about which specific thoughts may or may not be prosecutable may also be prosecutable.

[42.] (opposite) Scarfolk Books published an edition of the Bible, which was originally written many hundreds of years ago by people who had never heard of knives and forks, washing machines, toilet seats, shampoo and other sanitary products. The pages of the enhanced Scarfolk Bible were fitted with small sensors that worked much like a polygraph test. The sensors detected unconscious anxiety in the reader and, assuming it to be an indicator of wrongdoing or guilt, released a powerful electric shock. This edition's slogan was, 'Get a bit of tomorrow's Judgement Day today.'

[43.] Seven tourists visited that summer. Oddly, they were all called Timothy, wore identical clothes, and appeared to communicate with each other telepathically. Everyone called them 'The Tim Seven'. Three days after they arrived, all the birds disappeared and for months afterwards, whenever Scarfolk residents tried to use their telephones all they could hear on the other end was distant, frantic backward birdsong. 'The Tim Seven' also claimed they could psychically channel a long-dead Scarfolk resident – a fifteenth-century plague doctor called Ranlyn Spangles – but they could only pick up his thoughts that referred to wigs and bed socks.

A fleet of specially-designed vans, driven by teams of council-trained telepathic eunuchs, was sent out into the community to unmask people guilty of thinking prohibited thoughts. The scheme not only successfully reduced the number of telepathic crimes in Scarfolk, but also rooted out hundreds of 'wrong thinkers'.

As Daniel had surmised from personal experience, Scarfolk Council had 'bugged every room, every street; every public and private space. Even forests, beaches and bouncy castles were wiretapped. Every moment of every resident's life was recorded and archived in vast, secret bunkers.'[44] However, illicitly and unconstitutionally spying on a whole town required an enormous amount of taxpayers' money. That is why, in 1973, Scarfolk initiated a scheme to sell thought surveillance data back to the public. If one did not buy back one's own surveillance data, one risked the data – film and audio recordings – being sold to state-run television stations who broadcast the material to an audience hungry for acts of candid depravity. Shame and celebrity quickly became synonymous.

Finally, with fear (and confusion) gripping the community, and the council unable to keep track of what was and was not a criminal act,[45] a series of clever public information campaigns was launched that were nebulous enough for the citizens of Scarfolk to question and doubt their every move.

A characteristic example of these tactics is the 'Don't' public information campaign launched in 1973 and soon after followed by the 'Stop!' campaign.

The 'Stop!' campaign was directed at people who had, for whatever reason, failed to heed the pre-emptive 'Don't' campaign and recklessly begun to do something. For those whose acts of doing were either accidental or against their will (compulsively going upstairs, for example) there were teams of trained people-vets who helped wean the doer off their unlawful activity.

[44.] Daniel does not make the literal connection in his notes, but he must have wondered if these bunkers and those allegedly beneath the council building were one and the same.

[45.] Daily newspapers, which reported frequent and random changes in law, were updated every 3 minutes and anyone possessing an out-of-date edition was arrested, prosecuted for dissent and declared a Scarfnot. Books were also constantly rewritten and 'unbook' tokens were available. These tokens could be exchanged for any given book's amended pages. Indeed, some books were corrected so frequently that maintaining a single book could run into hundreds if not thousands of pounds. A book's contents could change drastically. For example, by 1979, the erotic sci-fi thriller *Affordable Brothel of the 9th Moon of Jupiter* bore little resemblance to its first edition, originally titled *A Beginner's Guide to Knitting & Crocheting*. Most people found it easier not to buy or read books, which may have been an intention of the council in the first place.

A poster for the 'Don't' campaign, featuring Kak the bird, the campaign's mascot. The council became increasingly concerned that citizens were too actively involved in 'doing' generally. Because 'doing' is a morally and politically ambiguous activity the council decided to take control and enforced 'not doing' until they could clarify and ratify only positive, socially acceptable expressions of 'doing'.

A 'Don't' costume worn by parents, dentists and school teachers.

A 'Don't' badge.

The 'Stop!' public information campaign. The posters were eventually withdrawn because hundreds of people, unsure what to do, would stand still on the street in front of the posters.

Opposite: A page from a council booklet that helped citizens understand the differences between the 'Don't' and 'Stop!' campaigns.

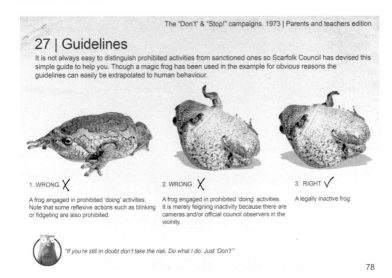

27 | Guidelines

It is not always easy to distinguish prohibited activities from sanctioned ones so Scarfolk Council has devised this simple guide to help you. Though a magic frog has been used in the example for obvious reasons the guidelines can easily be extrapolated to human behaviour.

1. WRONG. X

A frog engaged in prohibited 'doing' activities. Note that some reflexive actions such as blinking or fidgeting are also prohibited.

2. WRONG X

A frog engaged in prohibited 'doing' activities. It is merely feigning inactivity because there are cameras and/or official council observers in the vicinity.

3. RIGHT √

A legally inactive frog.

"If you're still in doubt don't take the risk. Do what I do: Just 'Don't'"

78

For those who blatantly flouted both the 'Don't' and 'Stop!' laws there was a zero tolerance policy: council-appointed barber-surgeons and plague doctors combed the streets for offenders.

Mayor Ritter might be dismissed by most as a typically overbearing council mayor, who only had the welfare of Scarfolk's residents at heart. But Daniel was not quite so charitable. He distrusted Ritter and called him a 'fiendish scoundrel, diabolical rapscallion and all-round twat'. Most importantly Daniel unequivocally writes across a ripped photocopy of a council report,'LTR [L.T. Ritter] MUST know the whereabouts of Joe and Oliver. I am convinced he is the key.'

The report itself is innocent enough. It addresses the number of bottles of free milk and packs of chocolate lice delivered to schools for children's playtimes[46] in the year 1970-71, but in doing so it inadvertently reveals a foreboding statistic. According to town records there were 3756 children attending Scarfolk schools in early 1970, but only 2890 a year later. Even with the 200 pupils who graduated that leaves a child deficit of exactly 666 children.

[46.] Free milk for school children was eventually abolished by Margaret Thatcher who consequently earned the moniker, 'The milk snatcher and inhuman death-sucking horror-witch who plundered a generation's hopes and dreams'.

The leaflet was another attempt to clarify to the public what was expected of them.

As we have learned, Ritter did not become mayor until 1 January 1970, but Daniel found information about him that sounded a much deeper truth. Who was L.T. Ritter and where did he come from? Even Daniel was surprised by his findings.

In the introduction I referred to the puzzling name of 'Ritel' that appeared in the Domesday Book of 1086CE in connection to a town called 'Scarefolke'. Who or what it referred to was never known. However, Daniel uncovered another, albeit tenuous reference to a 'Ritel' connected to Scarfolk, namely in a play by the Elizabethan playwright Thomas Clapfancy-Spincock,[47] who, in his 1592 tragedy *Death of a Fudge-maker's Goose*, wrote: 'Away with thy gnashing spimbles, thy unfriendly quill demons, thy Ritel that scareth folke.'

This is the last we hear of either 'Ritel' or 'Scar(e)-folk(e)' for almost 200 years. Then between 1793 and the 1930s there are two small, albeit tantalising references to a 'Ritel' in connection to the town: two signatures, both pointing to one person – the mayor of 1970s Scarfolk. In both cases the mayor spells his name differently: 'Ritalin Linkchard' and 'Retard de Lentil'. Written below each name in parenthesis is the title 'mayor of Scarfolk'. The signatures (both of which seem to be written by the same hand) appear on a 1793 invoice for 1000 mantraps and 3500 'tinctures for the vanquishment of Rabies' and a 1930 restraining order preventing 'de Lentilre' from performing magic within 200 feet of a specified cow on a Lancashire farm.[48]

[47.]Thomas Clapfancy-Spincock (1570-1603).Two other works are extant,*What I Did On My Holiday* (1576) and the medical/biological work *Treatise on the Human Head* (1603) which was published posthumously after the author, who believed humans did not medically require a head to survive, tried (successfully) to remove his own, having attached it by rope to a skittish racehorse.

[48.]The farm has been closed for many years and I cannot trace the original owners.The cow itself became the major ingredient in frozen cottage pies sold by a large supermarket chain and even a highly trained animal medium could not made contact.

Scarfolk Council
MEMORANDUM   -2-

To: ████████████████████   Date: June 6 ████

From: █████████████████████

To whom it may concern, Mrs ██████████████

████████████████████████████ mind your ---██████████
██
██
████████████ own ███████████████████████████████████
███████ fuc ██████████████████████████████ "King"
██
██
████████████████ business ███████████████████████████
██
OK? ██

signed:

████████ (for Mayor Ritter's office)

Daniel does not say how he came by this memo. Was the recipient Mrs Payne?

Is this mayor the same 'L.T. Ritter,' the 1970s' mayor of Scarfolk? And is a connection between this Ritter and the fearsome 'Ritel' in both 11th- and 16th-century England possible, or are they just coincidences? It seems inconceivable that one family, much less one individual, could snake its way throughout the history of Scarfolk. At this point, Daniel reached an impasse in his investigations:

> I needed help; I could no longer do it alone. Though I had become accustomed to carefully averting my eyes for fear of giving away my mental clarity, I was convinced that Mrs Payne had detected my reversion to the cognisant Daniel Bush who had arrived in Scarfolk. I also suspected she knew I'd seen the real Joe and Oliver in the fair that day. She was my only hope, but I had no way of knowing how she would react if I confronted her directly.

Daniel patiently waited several weeks until he was alone with Mrs Payne in the bungalow. The Joe and Oliver impostors were attending their weekly junior taxidermy club meeting at the local old people's home and Dr Hushson was, for once, not making one of his all too regular visits.

> I feigned tiredness and asked if I could go to bed early. She consented and while she prepared the thought-recording Sketch-a-Sketch device, she sang my favourite lullaby.

> > Wrinkle, wrinkle, little scar
> > I wonder just how deep you are
> > Down into my flesh so low
> > Without a blade I'll never know.

> When she had hooked me up to the Sketch-a-Sketch for my nightly surveillance recording, I did not hold back my thoughts; I permitted them to flow freely...

It must have been a great relief to Daniel, having concealed the contents of his mind for so long, to be finally able to express himself openly.[49]

> Before long, ghostly grey lines appeared on the Sketch-a-Sketch screen. My first question was: 'Are my sons alive?' Mrs Payne froze, panic flushed her face. She sat for a long moment saying nothing, teetering between blurting out the truth and rushing from the room. Sensing the latter I emitted another thought: 'Don't be afraid. I know Mayor Ritter is the bad man.' Mrs Payne finally responded with a small almost imperceptible nod.
>
> Another Sketch-a-Sketch message: 'Take me to them… please.'
>
> Again she sat for a moment before snatching the Sketch-a-Sketch, erasing my questions and then stating in a loud voice, no doubt for the many hidden microphones, 'the recording equipment is faulty. I request a replacement.' Then she stood to leave, but before she closed the door behind her she turned back to me and said, in the same consciously bright voice, 'Of course I'll take you to the zoo, Daniel. I know how much you like the elephants and goats and… what is it that comes after them? I don't remember now, but we'll see on Sunday after your stationery lesson, won't we?'
>
> I was stunned, elated. Mrs Payne was agreeing to help me. Were Joe and Oliver at the Outsiders' Zoo & Slaughter Gardens?

Daniel's notes indicate that he had visited the zoo several times before with Mrs Payne, Dr Hushson and his impostor sons/brothers. He was well aware, as were most citizens, that outsiders and tourists routinely found themselves in animal enclosures and/or vanished never to be seen again. Daniel strongly suspected that their discarded body parts were recycled into

---

[49.] Daniel was not the first person to have used the Sketch-a-Sketch in this way. It was also used by teachers to communicate with children who had become demon-possessed during kindergarten séances and by spiritualist tax inspectors who tracked down deceased citizens who owed outstanding income tax.

zoo merchandising: children considered themselves lucky if, in the stuffing of soft toy lions, box jellyfish and bacteria cells, they found a replacement hip joint or tooth filling.

> Even if Joe and Oliver were at the zoo and had survived this long why would Mrs Payne state our intention to visit the zoo loud enough for the surveillance equipment to pick it up?

Daniel quickly comprehended that her words must have been encoded and her true intention was to misdirect whoever was surveilling them. It was several hours before the answer to the puzzle finally presented itself to him. She had asked what comes after elephants and goats. On a standard Scarfolk transport map, there are two stations on the Murder Line, one called Elephant & Garfunkel, the other Goat Lord Quay, so when Mrs Payne asked, 'What comes after them?' she was not referring to another zoo animal but to the next stop on the line: Black Heart Lane, the location of the Scarfolk Council building.

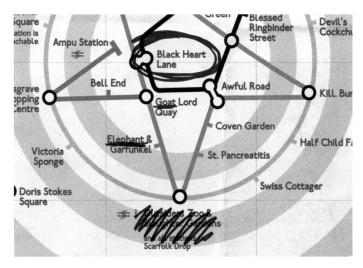

Scarfolk Transportation Map, Detail.

On the Run

THE NEXT DAY, as I filed stationery, I could hardly contain my anxiety and went to great lengths to compound the cover story: I enthused to the brother/son impostors about my impending zoo visit; to Dr Hushson too, who visited to administer my daily medication which I was still secretly hiding.

As soon as my chores were complete, I rushed to the train station. I was followed, of course, so I stood on the platform for the train that would take me to the zoo. When my pursuer was satisfied that I was taking the appropriate train he left and I slipped away and got on the train to Black Heart Lane.

When I arrived I waited for Mrs Payne just inside the station concourse not wanting to announce my presence so conspicuously. After 30 minutes she had not arrived. Nor had she after an hour. After one hour and 45 minutes, I knew she wasn't coming.

Had she betrayed me?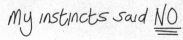

I was about to leave when I spied several people surreptitiously working their way towards me, Dr Hushson among them. He forced a well-practiced, benevolent smile as he produced a hypodermic needle from his pocket. Somewhere in the distance there was a sound that turned my blood cold: the sound of bells. Bells of the Morris...

I fled into the station. I could hear the jumbled footsteps of my pursuers striking the tiled floor behind

Mrs Payne at Scarfolk Fields

The inclusion in Daniel's archive of this Mrs Payne postcard and other gift-shop artefacts, which almost seem to revel in her demise, allude to her fate, no doubt at the hands of the cult.

me. The platforms were packed and I became entangled in commuters. I didn't have time to think; I leapt onto the tracks and ran clumsily along them. Ahead were three tunnels, all framed by signs warning of the physical harm that would befall anyone foolish enough to enter. I was about to change direction when an image of the gypsy woman from my recurring dreams flashed in my mind. She held up three fingers. There was no time for contemplation: I ran headlong into the darkness of tunnel three. My pursuers followed suit. Every noise I made was amplified and brought my pursuers ever closer.

I ducked into a narrow alcove and struggled to stifle my laboured breathing. Hushson called out to me and said something about my suffering from delusions and hallucinations after contracting rabies from a feral guinea pig that had run amok in Scarfolk.[50]

One by one torches came on. I retreated deeper into the alcove. I stumbled again, this time over an iron bar, which I realised was the top rung of a ladder that led down into unknown depths. As the beams of torch light stretched along the wall of the alcove towards me I realised I had no choice; I gripped the ladder and climbed down.

It took me several minutes to reach the bottom. I briefly stopped to cock an ear, but heard no indication that I was still being followed. I groped my way along a wall until I found a door, which opened onto a vast

Opposite: A health and safety placard. To tackle workplace accidents, Scarfolk Council adopted the principle behind vaccination, whereby a small amount of a virus is introduced to the body so that it builds up immunity. For example, to prepare for the eventuality of falling from the roof of a seven-storey office building, an employee, during a drill, would be thrown out of a low first-floor window. In the case of a gas leak explosion, which could kill fifty people, only three employees would be terminated during the drill.

[50.] Animals afflicted by unfriendly diseases and running amok was a common occurrence in Scarfolk. In 1972 an unwell spider went berserk, trashed a pub and stole a car, which it crashed into a greasy spoon café; and in 1970 four feverish snails cast off their shells and streaked at a football match (an event which contributed to the Scarfolk sports ban).

IN CASE OF AN EMERGENCY
or other emergencies

Main office building
& staff coven

1.

Hide under a beach towel or historically accurate cape.

2.

Rub a magic, high protein infant on a sacrificial prayer pig.

8.

Make a baby whoopsie on part-time employees.

6.

Hypnotise panicking colleagues with complicated shoe sole patterns

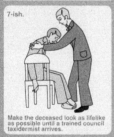

7-ish.

Make the deceased look as lifelike as possible until a trained council taxidermist arrives.

1. Follow the yet to be printed signs to wherever the exits will be built.

2. Though arrows point in the direction indicated by the directional point of the arrow, the direction indicated may not be an accurate indication of the appropriate direction.

3. Shouting, yelling or screaming for help will be viewed as attention-seeking and ignored.

4. Don't.

5. To report an emergency or seek help call 0413-343 (unattended during emergencies & seances).

6. IMPORTANT: Point profess your excellency seat outwards on.

7. For more information please reread.**

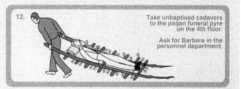

12.

Take unbaptised cadavers to the pagan funeral pyre on the 4th floor.

Ask for Barbara in the personnel department.

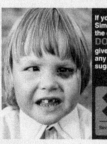

If you meet Simon in the corridor DO NOT give him any more sugar.

Severe Irritant

Do not anger the WWI ghost

Painless meat not warn victims in advance

All accidents will be televised

Get your burns, earthquake and terror act vaccinations

* Employees are strongly encouraged to improvise their own safety guidelines.

The emergency doors on all floors are just paintings.

There are no exits.

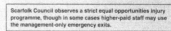

Scarfolk Council observes a strict equal opportunities injury programme, though in some cases higher-paid staff may use the management-only emergency exits.

** If you cannot read please learn to read before reading (or rereading) this document.

in

IAN PHLEGMY'S

THE MAN WITH THE STAPLE GUN

starring

CHARLES GRAPE

as

MR JOHNSON

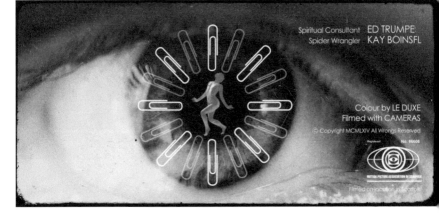

Spiritual Consultant ED TRUMPE
Spider Wrangler KAY BOINSFL

Colour by LE DUXE
Filmed with CAMERAS

© Copyright MCMLXIV All Wrongs Reserved

network of corridors, a maze of locked doors and empty
rooms constructed and decorated in a mishmash of cold
Victorian tiling and the minimal style of a modern office
building.

Televisions in cages were affixed to the walls, their
volumes were set high enough for the internal speakers
to vibrate and distort. They only played children's cartoons,
documentaries. and public information films, all propaganda
for the Officist cult. There were also feature films, which
referred at length to the worship of a monstrous 'horned
deity' called Mr Johnson.

If the programmes' narrations were any indication of Joe's and Oliver's fates,
they had either been sacrificed or chosen to represent the cult in the outside
world. The high production values of the Officist feature films suggested to
Daniel that the cult had wealthy, influential backers.

I was quickly lost. By the end of the first day I had
investigated almost 100 rooms varying in size from that of
a cupboard, areas as large as football pitches and spaces
so enormous I could not determine their size or even if
they had walls and ceilings.[51] I took any clues I could find,
such as signs and notices, from the walls and doors.

Daniel felt a modicum of reassurance when he found one room containing
an enormous pencil sharpener, which he recognised from his research
into the council building (see page 38). At least he knew where he was:
in the council's mysterious bunker complex. But his relief was short-lived:
he became aware that someone or something was following him.

*Opposite: Daniel somehow managed to track down these frames from the clearly big-
budget Officist feature* The Man With The Staple Gun.

[51.] Only the names Daniel attributed to some of the rooms give any indication
of what was contained within: 'the marmalade spider room', 'waste paper and
liver', 'the room of horrid trumps', 'the disembodied children's backwards choir',
'Hangman game-show TV studio'. He describes that he had to pass cautiously
through one carpeted room called 'Zombie donkey theatre' for fear of rousing the
cheerily decorated, volatile pleasure-beach equines from their undead stupor.

> It sounded large, hulking, like a bull wearing polyester
> trousers and clogs. I tried to avoid it, but the echoing
> corridors made its location hard to determine.[52]

At the end of a five-mile long corridor Daniel discovered a vast chamber that to him was the most disturbing. In an otherwise empty dark space, Daniel found, in the centre of the room, lit by spotlights, the remainder of his material life:

> The van I had travelled to Scarfolk in was coated in a
> layer of dust and the tyres were flat. I rolled up the rusted
> back and went through my, Joe's, and Oliver's possessions,
> just as I had packed them. I even found my medication
> that I had lost. It was long past its use-by-date, but I took
> it anyway partly out of hunger.[53]

As Daniel inspected the room further he found plinths holding objects: toys from his own childhood; his wedding ring; dozens of photographs from his entire life.

> Have they always been there in the shadows, one step
> behind me with cameras, with tape recorders?

Daniel did not have long to contemplate the meaning of the absurd exhibition because the entity that had been pursuing him had caught up.

> Its heavy breath and hooves were all around me. And
> there was the tinkling sound of paperclips and staples
> landing on the hard floor. I glimpsed a flash of horn in
> a shaft of light.

This is the first instance in Daniel's notes where he names his pursuer, confirming his belief that the Officist cult was responsible not only for the abduction of his children, but also, in some way, for the death of his wife, Joy.

Apparently, this sign often accompanied safety notices that had more than a line or two of text.

---

52. Daniel's account is reminiscent of the ancient Greek story of Theseus and the Minotaur, which is based on an earlier tale about a hero called Gareth from Ages Ago. It is fortunate that the Greeks eventually developed dramaturgical arts because the original leaves a lot to be desired: 'One day Gareth lost his favourite ball of string. He could not find it no matter where he looked. He went to the local farmer and asked if he had seen it, but the farmer said he had not. Gareth asked the local butcher if he had seen his string, but he had not seen it either. Finally, Gareth asked his mother if she had seen his ball of string. She asked him if he had checked his pocket. Gareth did so and found the string.'

53. As described previously, the side-effects of Lobottymed (and withdrawal from it) can include mental aberrations. But what about side-effects produced by out-of-date medication? At the time of writing this book, there was no information available. However, we do know about a similar drug, Litigappease, which Cavalier Pharm administered to people who had been traumatised by earlier mishandled medical trials. Litigappease was designed to cauterise the area of the brain that deals with aggrieved feelings and the desire for litigation. However, it also severely affected speech, memory and motor skills, thus, tragically, the ability to make sandwiches.

It had to be Mr Johnson. It was inevitable. Terrified, I ran blind into the darkness, Mr Johnson's hooves behind me accelerating first into a trot, then a sort of sloppy tango, then a relentless gallop.

Just as my legs began to lock from exhaustion, searing pain exploded in my face. I was catapulted backwards as if I'd been struck squarely on the nose with a shovel.[54]

I had collided with a metal door. My nose was broken and I could taste blood but there was something else: my mouth was filling with paper discs: the waste product of an office hole-puncher. I yanked and shook the door handle. It was jammed. Mr Johnson was gaining on me. I struggled with the stubborn door, desperate to get purchase. As Mr Johnson's hooves slowed to a standstill and I felt his breath in my hair, the door latch finally gave. I flung the door open and slipped out into the cold night, slamming the door shut behind me.

Daniel writes about his pursuer as if he truly were the primeval, mythical being of Officist legend. Could it be that his overactive journalist's mind, accompanied by the out-dated medication and the literature he had compiled about the Scarfolk Beast had compounded his sense of unreality? I have no doubts whatsoever that Daniel got lost in the Scarfolk bunker complex and that it was an unsettling experience, though him finding his worldly possessions is perhaps too convenient, a case of wishful thinking in a moment of panic when he so desperately needed something, anything familiar to grasp on to.

Lastly, this is the only time in Daniel's notes that he describes such an immediate interaction with Mr Johnson/the Scarfolk Beast, so we are left to draw our own conclusions. I believe that other rational explanations for Mr Johnson's presence are open to us. For example, I postulate the following: a mentally-ill cow accidentally wanders in from the street. It lives undetected in the bunkers for many years and learns how to stand upright by reading emergency exit diagrams and safety notices from which it also learns rudimentary first aid. Sensing that Daniel is in distress and weakened by hunger, the cow chases after him, keen to practise its new-found medical skills and its unique ability to stand on two legs. In short, Daniel's frightening encounter could have been considerably reduced if a psychologically unbalanced, precocious bovine had not wanted to show off.

These signs were recreated according to rough sketches made by Daniel during his time in the bunker complex.

---

54. Taking the average running speed of 6 miles per hour, I invited two groups of men of Daniel's age and approximate weight to run headlong into a) a steel door b) the path of a man wielding a standard garden spade. The results demonstrated that injuries sustained by the spade group were far greater than those by door collisions, leading me to the conclusion that all of Daniel's post-Lobottymed descriptions are imprecise by approximately 8.75%. This should be taken into consideration.

Reunited

WHAT FOLLOWS ARE the final notes from Daniel Bush's archive. From the moment he arrived in Scarfolk on 23 December 1970, everything that had occurred to him led to this moment and this place, outside the council building, out of breath and out of time.

I lay in the wet grass in a small park area behind the council building struggling for breath. It was dark. The sound of chanting was coming from a candle-lit, ground-floor council room. A pale blue light swept the ceiling of one ground floor room – a photocopier[55] operating somewhere out of sight. *MRJ?*

I crept to the window. Dozens of swaying townspeople were gathered in a wide circle. I recognised several of them: PC Lyre, Quimpy waitress Diane Heidem, Dr Hushson and Mr Rumbelows/Dixon Currys who was eyeing the legs of a tall woman I did not know.

There, in the middle of the gathering, were two boys, or rather young men, with their backs to me. About 17 or 18 years old, they were elegantly dressed in tailored suits, their hairstyles coiffed just so. They appeared at ease amid the assembly. A middle-aged woman, taken up in the moment and obviously very proud, couldn't resist breaking the circle to kiss the boys' cheeks. When the boys turned I saw at once that they were Joe and Oliver.

[55.] I found a reference to 'MRJ Range' in a 1979 book about the history of office equipment called *Imprinting Behaviours* published by the Klofracs Publishing Company. The entry for the photocopier is missing but the range's printer is of particular interest: 'The MRJ01 printer, also known as an Empath Printer, had the ability to print the user's thoughts without him having to write them down first. Though the new machine reduced costs of night-office children, it began printing what it believed users should be writing rather than what the user intended or even wanted. It was discontinued when two of the printers at a school textbook publisher

I called out their names but none of the gathering responded. I was about to rap on the window but something happened that transfixed me, something indelible. A man and a woman entered the room, led by Morris dancers, to join the mayor and boys in the middle of the circle.

I immediately recognised the man as myself: Daniel Bush. The woman was my dead wife, Joy.

I scrutinised her for any sign of fakery; like Joe and Oliver she was a few years older, but she was unmistakably Joy. Not only did I recognise myself, I also felt a disjointed pang of déjà vu.[56] It was as if I were faintly remembering what the me inside the room was experiencing as it was happening. This convinced me that the other me and Joy could not possibly be impostors.

The me inside the room shook each of the boys' hands in turn while Joy kissed and hugged them to a round of applause. It was then that I noticed for the first time that the entire Bush family moved stiffly and that they were all missing a left leg below the knee.

I was overcome by profound feelings of guilt and I could not rid myself of the notion that I was responsible for everything that had happened. I ran from my place outside the window around the council building to the wide, double front doors. I flung them open and ran inside, my sole goal being to disrupt the uncanny proceedings and to flee with my family.

---

55 contd. began printing letters to all human employees informing them that they had been made redundant.' By chance, I have an MRJ01 printer in my office. It is still functional and I have not known it to perform in any unconventional way. I even used it to print a draft manuscript of this book.

56. 'Déjà vu' comes from the French and is literally translated as: 'Time having to go through the rigmarole of repeating itself because you were not paying enough attention or were too lazy to notice it the first time around.'

But as I neared the sacred standing stone in the council foyer I[57] was struck by a sickening dizziness. I pushed on but the nausea increased. The stone itself was repelling me and though I fought against it, the stone's unseen force prevailed and I blacked out.

ONE OF THE STONE'S SYMBOLS

When I regained consciousness I was shivering. Sand was in my mouth and water lapped at my feet. The cries of seagulls echoed against steep cliff walls. I was on a beach in the popular seaside town of Water-upon-Sea,[58] 95 miles from Scarfolk. In the fine spray of distant, crashing waves I could see Mr Johnson. I could tell by his stance that he had no intention of giving chase. Indeed, he turned, dropped his half-eaten ice-cream cone, and headed in the direction of the amusement arcades.

[57.] See also page 46.

[58.] Water-upon-Sea is popular for its second shoreline, which hovers some 170 feet above the first and is accessible only by ladder. The seaside resort is also notorious for what is known as the 'Water-upon-Sea Icosidodecadodecahedron' – an area that many claim is a hotspot of supernatural activity. In addition to the sudden appearance of estranged family members (see pages 32/33), in 1976 a UFO allegedly landed in the car park of the town's supermarket. The ship's occupant was seen purchasing several bottles of cheap German Riesling, a selection of cream cakes and a Demis Roussos cassette, leading paranormal experts to postulate that the otherworldly visitor might have been going through an unhappy break-up.

Complete with full colour photos of black & white illustrations

CHUCK BERLIN

the water-upon-sea icosidodecad- odecahedron

The bestselling saga of unexplaineded unexplainedables

The Water-upon-Sea Icosidodecadodecahedron *by Chuck Berlin, Bantam Books, 1975.*

It took Daniel two days to return to Scarfolk. During the journey he scribbled many pages of notes, committing to paper his memory of the events while they were fresh in his mind.

> It was night when I arrived. I rushed directly to the
> council building. The entrance doors were locked so I
> returned to the window at the rear. The same event was
> occurring; not the festivities in general, but the identical
> sequence of events: the proud middle-aged woman kissing
> the boys, Mayor Ritter putting his arm around the boys'
> shoulders; the other me and Joy entering the circle to first
> shake the hands of the boys then hug them.
>
> I slammed my palm repeatedly against the window
> pane. They couldn't hear me. It was if I were outside time.
> There was only one discernible change in the sequence of
> the events as I had seen them previously. Mayor Ritter
> turned to face me. We briefly made eye contact before he
> turned away again. His eyes were emotionless, dead, like
> he was erasing me.
>
> I ran around the building desperate to find a way in. I
> tried to scramble through a narrow open window but was
> met by a familiar wave of light-headedness.[59]
>
> I understood then that what- or whoever was blocking
> my entry, could not be overcome. I was as frustrated and
> resigned as I was nauseous.
>
> I made my way back through SCarfolk
> to the now empty bungalow. The cameras and cables were all gone. It
> appeared to have been unoccupied for years. I feared that my archive
> of papers would be gone, but it was still below the floorboard where I
> had hidden it. I stuffed as many pages into my clothes as I could, then
> set off into the night.

Though these are the last words we have from Daniel Bush himself, they are not the final word in our investigation of Scarfolk.

[59.] Nausea at the site of sacred stones is not uncommon. Children who were about to be sacrificed on altars hewn from such stones often reported unexpected, unaccountable feelings of apprehension and general nervousness.

SCARFOLK PUBLIC TRANSPORT
For public transport in Scarfolk

When you leave Scarfolk you leave a piece of yourself behind*

Single and one-way tickets available from the ticket office in the main station

*Mandatory donation

When leaving Scarfolk please take your dirty litter & other family members with you

A Scarfolk public transport poster, 1970s.

Final Words

THERE IS ONE outstanding piece of evidence that I can add to Daniel's story. On 31 December 1979, an agitated man filed a report with police in the town of Easeby, not far from where Daniel claims Scarfolk was located. He reported a series of crimes including kidnapping, false imprisonment, torture and being taken by supernatural means to a delightful seaside resort against one's will. A police psychiatrist was called, but she never got to interview the distraught man because he fled before she arrived. I intentionally refer detachedly to the man because, according to the police report, the person who filed the accusations was not called Daniel Bush. His name was Joseph Oliver.

EASEBY POLICE STATEMENT		DATE	31/12/1979		
		CASE, NUMBER	08 2987		
NAME OF VICTIM	Joseph Oliver	AGE ?	OFFENCE	kidnapping/torture	
FAVOURITE COLOUR	Unknown	GENDER M	DATE OF OFFENCE	Dec 1970 - 31 Dec 1979	
			LOCATION OF OFFENCE	Scarfolk (?. - town unknown)	

Having pored over this archive and seen for myself the extraordinary lengths to which its author and curator went to preserve the events he claims to have endured, it is hard to believe that he would have identified himself as anyone other than Daniel Bush.

Why the name Joseph Oliver should appear on the police report is not known. Perhaps the officer on duty that night had been celebrating the New Year with fellow officers and mistook the boys' names for the name of the accuser. Perhaps he had suffered a brain injury as a child after trying to lick a fox or an electricity pylon.

Whatever the man's name, he was unquestionably the person whose account I have presented in this book. I largely omitted only repetitions and unconnected details, such as those that refer to a spate of exploding terrorist kittens and a portal in the post office's passport photo-booth, which allegedly permitted time travel to anyone bearing the correct denomination of stamps.[60]

Did all of these events truly occur? In the absence of further tangible evidence you may feel you have no choice but to make a decision based on gut feeling, or ignorance, as it is sometimes known. Alternatively, you may refuse to adhere to any one theory and conclude that the truth will never be known. But remember this: it is crucially important whether or not these events occurred. We cannot afford to be agnostic about the systematic kidnapping and abuse of children (and adults) and the wanton ill-treatment of shire horses with inner ear disorders.

In my opinion, there are three possible readings of the evidence: 1) Daniel Bush's archive is a complex forgery, the product of a playful desire to fool the world. In many ways I hope that this is the case and that, somewhere out there, Daniel and his sons are wryly grinning to themselves. 2) Daniel fabricated the archive but convinced himself that it represented reality after suffering a mental collapse.[61] If this did occur, we are faced with one important question: Where are Joseph and Oliver Bush? Why have they not come forward to clarify their father's mental state during the 1970s and, more importantly, why is there no official record of them after Daniel took them out of school to lead a new life up north? It does not bear thinking about, but we must entertain the idea that Daniel invented his experiences as a means to cope with something he did to his own boys; something so wicked and traumatising that it warranted the concoction of an elaborate alternative reality.[62]

We are left with the final hypothesis, that everything occurred just as Daniel claimed. To accept the veracity of his archive is to accept that

---

[60.] According to Daniel, the photo-booth, which only permitted travel within the 1970s, was always guarded and he never used it: 'A trip costs £2.95 first class, £1.75 second class (though this can take up to 30 days to arrive, which is useless if you only wanted to time travel a few hours or days in time). You should always write your return address on one buttock in case you get lost. Also, do not forget to include a stamped, self-addressed envelope or you will not be returned.'

supernatural and totalitarian forces were at work in 1970s England; that there was an official and blatant policy of erasing outsiders; that citizens were routinely spied upon by their own government and flagrantly exploited by ruthless corporations; that children were subjected to illicit drug trials, their bodies disfigured because of fads in medicine unsupported by rigorous scientific research.

Could it really be true that these outrages were permitted in a civilised modern society? Could they happen today? Surely not. And yet Daniel's archive unequivocally states that these things transpired and in abundance, beneath our very noses.

At the centre of Daniel's claims is a cult obsessed by office supplies with a desire to place its members, voluntary or otherwise, in positions of societal

---

61. (previous) Other theories have been posited. I include them here but see no reason to investigate them further.

1) Daniel experienced a collapse in the space-time continuum during an otherwise innocent holiday in Water-upon-Sea: he experienced several reincarnations of himself at once, which not only lead to profound psychic confusion but also incurred an enormous tax bill.
2) Daniel had a telepathic cross-wiring and accidentally channelled several aliens who were doing a scientific survey of North Wales to find out whether or not life could be sustained there.
3) Daniel Bush, his family and story were fabricated by me, the author of this book, to make up for a failing academic career. As my department chair commented in a recent edition of *Academics' Wives* monthly magazine: 'Tenuring Motte was a mistake and I've regretted it since. Despite the recent, inexplicable circumstances which led to the loss a limb, for which I offer my sincere sympathy, Motte continues to be more devoted to his Morris dancing troupe than he does his academic work. His research lacks the rigorous intellectual insights expected of a member of this department's staff. I wouldn't be surprised to learn that he'd manufactured a whole body of research just to justify his position at this university. Pathetic.'

62. (previous) Theories about what Daniel may have done to his own sons include:

1) When he could not find his sons after accidentally losing them, he tried to psychologically mask his guilt by inventing a fictional antagonist: Scarfolk.
2) He heard an ice-cream van's jingle, which was reminiscent of the Morris dancing bells he heard during his wife's death. He had a psychotic episode, killed his own boys with a frozen lolly, buried them and never regained his sanity.
3) He inadvertently, and through no fault of his own, ate them.

influence. If this is true it is in our best interests to be in possession of all the facts. Some might advise we err on the side of caution and scrutinise any profession that relies heavily on stationery and office supplies: teachers, post office staff, office managers, politicians, civil servants, bankers, corporate leaders, police, information technologists, origami experts. If our leaders are indeed ushering us towards an obscure cult's apocalypse, we cannot allow this to unfold unnoticed.

Most importantly, if one day you find yourself in a car, or on a train or bus, and you encounter a sign that directs you towards a town called Scarfolk, it is imperative that you do everything within your means to steer clear of it. Some destinations were never meant to be reached, because once their secrets have been discovered they cannot be undiscovered.

For more information please reread this book.

Appendices

Appendix I / p.184
'Two Boys Disappear or Something'
Scarfolk Herald, published Thursday 24 December 1970

Appendix II / p.186
Patient report for Dixon Currys

Appendix III / p.187
Film: *It'll Have Your Eye Out*

The SBFC Report, 21 May 1978

The
Scarfolk Herald

Today's latest civic law and by-law amendments are printed on pages 12-46. Mr. Rumbelows from Scarfolk Council also discusses the latest punishments and reveals which are his favourites.

Edition 24 Vol 7474   Dec 24 1970   The Daily Newspaper That You Brings You Paper. Every Day.

TWO BOYS DISAPPEAR OR SOMETHING

Two boys have been reported missing by a man, perhaps the boys' father. The boys, named Julie (Joey?) and Oliver or Alan, or something like that, have not been seen since either yesterday or the day before. It's not the first time that tragedy has afflicted this family. The boys lost their mother earlier this year in mysterious circumstances.

By lost we do not mean misplaced. Presumably, the surviving family members know exactly where her body is buried. Assuming she wasn't cremated, of course.

→

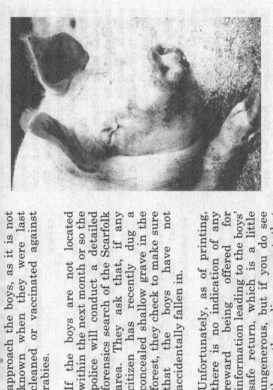

outside Scarfolk. This means that, should there be a tragic outcome, strictly speaking, the case does not fall under the jurisdiction of Scarfolk council. However, Scarfolk police have generously cut short their annual inter-station Buckaroo tournament to help in the search. Despite visiting most pubs in Scarfolk, they are yet to turn up any leads.

Police have asked anyone who was awake recently, and who is not too busy, to keep an eye out for the boys who answer the following description:

They are about the height of children with standard-issue child costumes. Both boys are male. Both have hair and other conventional attributes (see any regular child for further details) however, the smaller of the boys has a mole on his left kidney. One of the boys might be carrying a pig under one arm, though this is highly unlikely as neither boy owns a pig or has any access to pigs.

approach the boys, as it is not known when they were last cleaned or vaccinated against rabies.

If the boys are not located within the next month or so the police will conduct a detailed forensics search of the Scarfolk area. They ask that, if any citizen has recently dug a concealed shallow grave in the forest, they check to make sure that the boys have not accidentally fallen in.

Unfortunately, as of printing, there is no indication of any reward being offered for information leading to the boys' safe return, which is a little ungenerous, but if you do see them, the police request that you inform them whenever is convenient for you, but preferably before 9pm because they like to have a couple of nightcaps before bedtime.

We do not have the missing persons hotline number to hand, but you can fill out a 'crime solved' card at the library and pop it in the police station letter box.

Pre-mortem obituaries page 48

SCARFOLK
Country Club & Hospital
for the Mentally Fucked

LITTLE BOX WITH A TICK ☑
LITTLE BOX WITHOUT A TICK ☐
LITTLE BOX WITH AN AMBIGUOUS TICK ⧄

OFFICE USE ONLY

ᴵᴹPATIENT REPORT

PATIENT	Dixon Currys	DATE	
REF. #	45/B 765something67/X etc	DOCTOR	

SUMMARY:

Dixon continues to demonstrate his various manias and refuses all offers of cleansing staplegun blood-letting treatments. He still fervently believes that his legs are hindering him.

This may have something to do with his 32 separate full-time personalities with a further 2 that only appear at weekends, if they can get time off work. Believing he has 68 legs overwhelms Dixon, especially when he goes shopping for shoes.

My colleagues and I are convinced that, while most children benefit from it, Dixon did not respond well to being sellotaped by the legs to the underside of a Cessna aeroplane as a baby.

Psychologically, Dixon is approximately 9 years old and none of his other personalities have thought to tutor him in even the most rudimentary subjects such as Maths, English and Stationery Studies. Dixon is incapable of telling the difference between algebra and algae or a protractor and a tractor (which, incidentally, is why he spent several weeks in Scarfolk Infirmary recently).

However, his mental age means that he is good with children and we can use him as an intermediary when dealing with children we have traumatised in the bunkers. Furthermore, Dixon no longer has a tangible personality of his own; he is essentially a cypher to be 'programmed' at will like a computer or prole.

He can make no decisions of his own and is easily manipulated by other patients, particularly those afflicted equally by both clinical laziness and obsessive compulsive disorder, such as patient Jefferson who slouches for hours in front of the TV while coercing Dixon into compulsively touching all the clinic's wash basins for him.

SCARFOLK BOARD OF FILM CENSORS

3, HOSO SQUARE, W.I.

President: The Rt. Hon, L. T. RITTER
Secretary: JOHNNY FUDGE

Distributed by Scarfolk Public Films
Running Time: 2 mins 32 secs
Category: 'U'

21 MAY Date 1978

TITLE: "IT'LL HAVE YOUR EYE OUT"

SYNOPSIS:

The film starts with two young boys happily playing cowboys and indians on
wasteland. They try to climb over a wall covered in glass shards and
barbed wire. Boy A slips in his flip-flops and is lacerated by glass
before getting tangled in the wire. When he tries to move, a bird
defecates on him. Boy B screams. He kicks off his flip-flops and rushes to
help, but Boy A's expression has become one of dark malevolence. Only the
whites of his eyes are visible; there are no pupils. Boy B screams. He
turns and runs.

Boy B flees across open barren fields chased by rabid, snarling dogs,
frothing at the mouth. Several dark, menacing figures stand motionless on
the horizon. Not looking where he is going, Boy B suddenly crashes
headlong into a stove/oven, which is in the middle of the field. A hot pan
spills, the boy is burned by boiling liquid and the stove's hob flames are
extinguished. Gas hisses. Boy B writhes in the dirt. The ground gives way
beneath him. He screams as he falls into a sinkhole. His leg breaks on the
way down and juts out at a disquieting angle. He finds himself on an iced-
over pool, which begins to crack under his weight. He screams. The ice
gives way and Boy B finds himself in the dark, muddy water filled with
shopping trolleys, discarded refrigerators and other objects likely to
ensnare.

The dark figures stand at the lip of the hole and stare down at him but do
not help. Boy B screams. Rabid dogs snarl. Gas hisses. A crow caws (it's
not clarified in the film if this is the same bird that defecated on Boy
A). Boy B struggles to stay above the slimy surface but loses the battle
and goes under. His groping, grasping hands eventually find a rope.

CONTINUED.......

S-15.

Exerting himself he climbs and climbs and screams. Nearing the top of the hole the boy sees that the 'rope' is actually a loose cable from a nearby electricity pylon. He screams. There's a loud crack, a flash of electricity and the boy is hurled through the air. The smouldering boy flies over the leaking gas oven, which he ignites causing it to explode.

The boy smashes to the ground, breaking an arm, which juts out at a disquieting angle. He emits a scream but it is drowned out by the sound of a loud whistle and metallic screeching. The boy snaps his head up to see a speeding inter-city train bearing down on him. He realises he's on railway tracks. He screams. Aboard the train we see the mysterious dark figures, strange-eyed Boy A and the snarling dogs. Boy B screams. The screen goes black.

The film cuts to a scene of sullen Boy B sitting in a wheelchair in his bedroom. He has no legs and only one arm. In the background a woman's voice (probably his mother) can be heard saying, 'He's no use to anyone now. If they allowed it we'd have him put down. It's only fair.'

Inexplicably, a lit firework flies in through the open window and lands by the boy. It fizzes and sparks. The boy shouts for his mother, but she doesn't come. He tries blowing out the firework to no avail. Finally, he struggles to reach the firework and with his only hand picks it up. He throws it toward the open window but misses and the firework lands back beside him. He retrieves it and is about to throw it again when BANG, the firework explodes. The boy screams. We freeze on his agonised expression. Finally, there is a voice-over:

'Always make sure that you pay the proper postage for your letters, postcards and parcels. Visit your post office for more details.'

CONTINUED...

ASSESSOR'S COMMENTS:

If the filmmakers intended some form of cautionary message it's not apparent from either the film or the submitted script. The filmmakers are therefore to be applauded as this in itself is a valuable lesson for youngsters, adults with the minds of infants and northerners.

The following cuts/modifications are required for a 'U' certificate:

I. Both boys are blond. Unless you want to be accused of promoting white supremacy please change. Additionally, it might be more acceptable to a sensitive audience if the badly injured Boy B is coloured.

2. The term 'cowboys and indians' is outmoded and should be replaced with 'cattle herders and illegal prior occupants'.

3. The film contravenes guidelines on nudity, in that nudity does not feature anywhere in this film.

4. The rabid dogs are very frightening and must be softened. Please have the dogs wear yellow clogs or little hats, such as might be found in Christmas crackers.

5. Rabies can affect any animal. Using dogs exclusively might aggravate the Canine Rights Commission. We suggest mixing in a few other mammals such as fox, squirrel and manatee.

6. The boy grabbing the rope could be construed as an onanistic sexual act, especially as this is emphasised by the boy's slimy hands, exerted grunts and grimacing facial expression. We recommend that the boy climbs out of his own accord before being struck by the live electricity cable.

CONTINUED.......

143

7. The mysterious figures are strangely passive. Perhaps one of them could kick or slap Boy B.

8. The boy breaks a leg and an arm, both of which 'jut out at a disquieting angle', which we have assumed is greater than 90 degrees. This clearly contravenes the guidelines. The maximum break angle is 50.5 degrees. Only compound fractures may exceed this angle.

9. Flip-flops are too sexually provocative. Replace with shiny, rubber, black, knee-length wellington boots.

I0. In the shot of Boy B being hurled through the air, a dummy has obviously been used. Please use a real child or dwarf or the believability of the scenario may be significantly impaired.

II. In the final scene, Boy B's mother can be heard saying, 'He's no use to anyone now. If they allowed it we'd have him put down. It's only fair.' This is too callous. To lighten the tone, please change so that the mother is laughing as she delivers the line.

I2. Again, in the final scene, Boy B's injuries look like the work of a make-up effects department. Please either use an appropriately disabled actor or recreate the injuries in an able-bodied one.

END

IT'LL HAVE YOUR EYE OUT:
A PUBLIC INFORMATION TREASURY

THIS FILM HAS NOT BEEN PASSED

SCARFOLK BOARD
OF FILM CENSORS

3. HOSO SQUARE, SCARFOLK W.1.

President
The Rt. Hon. The Lord Ritter KCMG

PRESIDENT *L T Ritter*

Jimmy Fudge SECRETARY

Picture credits: Babies: 42-28863074 & 42-28865088: Corbis/©SuperStock (page 12). Tramps: 71780A - REX/SipaPress 3192634a: REX/Janine Wiedel (page 85).

The Penguin and Pelican logos and branding are the intellectual property of Penguin Books Limited and have been used in this book with their express permission.

Acknowledgements and thanks: Shirokazan; Evan-Amos; Wellcome Library, London; D Sharon Pruitt; Jay Aremac; M C Morgan; University of Haifa Younes & Soraya Nazarian Library; Britain Express Ltd; West Midlands Police; Biswarup Ganguly; Nevit Dilmen; London SE1 Community Website; Distillated; Sean MacEntee; Niki Odolphie; David Shankbone; Micky**; Smackandtoss, and the on-line community generally, for more information on which please visit the Scarfolk website http://scarfolk.blogspot.com/p/book. html; Ellie Wixon; Juliet Pickering and everyone at Blake Friedmann; Sarah Lavelle, Tim Bainbridge and everyone at Ebury Publishing; Dominic Cooper; David Eldridge; Tony Lyons; Will Mower; Tim Robinson; Burgberger Klausenverein. And to all the online civic-minded Scarfolkians who joined in and contributed their own mental commentaries. It's nice to know I'm not the only resident of Scarfolk.

Special thanks to Andrea, to whom this book is dedicated. I'm sorry for the many times I woke you at 5am to ask your opinion about the preferred method for damaging children and old people. Thank you for your tireless support.

WE W

YO

WHILE

SLE